"I'm not offering romance. I've been there, done that, and come out empty every time."

The edge of contempt in Nathan's voice startled Miranda into looking at him. "Look around you," he directed. "My life is bound up in this land. It comes down to basic needs, and that is pervasive if you live here long enough. I have a great respect for basic needs. And sharing them makes sense to me."

Miranda frowned, realizing he was talking of a stark reality she faced day after day.

"Now, I'd say there's something very basic between us that we could answer for each other. I'm not interested in the games men and women play in the world you come from," he said with an relentless beat that seemed to drum on her mind and heart. "I'll say it how it is for me. I want you, Miranda. And you want me."

Dear Reader,

Last year I chartered a plane to fly me from Broome, the pearling capital of the world, right across the Kimberly region of the great Australian outback. The vast plains are home to huge cattle stations, the earth holds rich minerals, and the outposts of civilization are few and far between. I wondered how people coped, living in such isolated communities.

"They breed them big up here," my pilot said. "It's no place for narrow minds, mean hearts or weak spirits. You take it on and make it work." He grinned at me. "And you fly. Can't do without a plane to cover the distances."

Yes, I thought. Big men. KINGS OF THE OUTBACK. Making it work for them. And so the King family started to take shape in my mind—one brother mastering the land, running a legendary cattle station; one who mastered the outback with flight, providing an air charter service; and one who mined its riches—pearls, gold, diamonds—selling them to the world.

Such men needed special women. Who would be their queens? I wondered. They have come to me, one by one—women who match these men, women who bring love into their lives, soul mates in every sense.

I now invite you to share the journeys of the heart for these KINGS OF THE OUTBACK. This is Nathan and Miranda's story. Tommy's will follow. Then Jared's. Three romances encompassing the timeless, primitive challenge of the Australian outback and a touch of what the Aboriginals call "The Dreamtime."

With love,

Emma Darcy

Emma Darcy

THE CATTLE KING'S MISTRESS

Kings of the
Outback

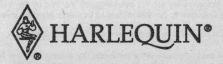

HARLEQUIN®

TORONTO • NEW YORK • LONDON
AMSTERDAM • PARIS • SYDNEY • HAMBURG
STOCKHOLM • ATHENS • TOKYO • MILAN • MADRID
PRAGUE • WARSAW • BUDAPEST • AUCKLAND

ISBN 0-373-12110-5

THE CATTLE KING'S MISTRESS

First North American Publication 2000.

Copyright © 2000 by Emma Darcy.

CHAPTER ONE

MISTRESS to a married man…no way!

Miranda realised she was gritting her teeth again and consciously relaxed her jaw. She'd end up grinding her teeth right down if she kept thinking of Bobby Hewson and his blithe assumption they could continue as lovers, his forthcoming marriage being no barrier whatsoever to what *they shared!*

Well, he could find someone else to warm his bed next time he flew into Sydney. Adultery was not her scene. She might have been a fool to have let Bobby play her along with promises for three years, but she was not going to be *used* for his extra-marital pleasure. She'd seen what that second-string kind of relationship had done to her mother. Never, never, never would she go down the same demeaning and destructive path!

"Miss Wade, your gin and tonic."

Miranda wrenched her mind off burning thoughts and looked up at the smiling airline hostess who proceeded to lay a serviette on the small metal drinks tray, which extended from the wide armrest of the first-class seat. A little bottle of gin, a can of tonic water and a glass with ice cubes were set down.

Nice to be treated to first-class service by her new employers, Miranda thought, and hoped the drink might help relax her. "Thank you," she said, returning the smile.

The hostess's eyes glowed with interest as she remarked, "I just noticed the book in your lap, *King's Eden*. Are you heading there?"

It was the book Elizabeth King had given her for background information, once Miranda had signed the two-year contract that tied her to managing the wilderness resort. A history of the place and the family who owned it might be dry reading, but mandatory in the circumstances, and the best use of these hours in flight to Darwin. Miranda sternly told herself it was time she concentrated on her future course and put the past in the past.

"Yes, I am," she answered, deciding to plumb the interest being displayed. "Do you know it?"

"I've been there," came the obviously enthusiastic reply. "It's what you might call a legendary place in the Kimberly, owned and run by the cattle Kings. Now that they've opened up the wilderness park for tourists and built a resort to cater for them, it's a very popular outback destination."

"Did you stay at the resort?"

"Not at the homestead." An expressive eye-roll. "Too expensive. A group of us stayed three days in the tented cabins at Granny Gorge."

Tented cabins, camping sites, bungalows and homestead suites—four levels of accommodation to be managed, Miranda reminded herself—a far cry from a five-star hotel. Was she mad to take it on…two years in the wilderness?

"Did you think it was worth the trip?" she asked the hostess.

"Oh, yes! Well worth it! I've never seen so many

butterflies. The trees around there were filled with them. And we swam in a gorgeous turquoise waterhole fed by waterfalls off the cliffs. Great way to have a shower.''

"So you'd definitely recommend it."

"To anyone," the hostess confirmed. "Don't miss the Aboriginal carvings in the caves if you go to the Gorge."

"I won't. Thank you."

Well, King's Eden had appealed to at least one person, Miranda noted as the hostess moved off. Its only appeal to her at the present moment, was the chance it offered to live her life on her own terms.

If she'd stayed with the Regency hotel chain, she might have moved from assistant manager in Sydney to an overseas posting, an ambition she'd once nursed, but it would have only happened now if she'd also stayed sweet with Bobby. He'd made that clear, offering steps up the managerial ladder as a persuader to win her compliance with his marriage, which, he'd argued, was only for the purpose of cementing an alliance between two great international hotel chains.

Another lie!

The photograph of his French fiancée in the newspaper was more than enough proof to Miranda that Bobby would find his honeymoon no hardship at all.

He'd obviously been lying to her all along—three years of lies. The only thing she'd ended up believing was his threat to stop her getting a decent position anywhere else if she walked out on him. It was sickeningly clear he'd do and say anything to get his own way.

King's Eden offered her the perfect escape from that

kind of victimisation. It was a one-off resort complex, not linked to anything or anyone that Bobby Hewson could touch or influence.

She smiled grimly as she recalled one of the questions Elizabeth King had asked at the interview.

"You are...unattached?"

*De*tached, Miranda had almost answered, barely swallowing her bitterness over Bobby's sleazy propositions and manipulations. "I am completely free, Mrs King," she had stated. "My life is very much my own."

And that was how it was going to be at King's Eden, Miranda vowed. Her own life run by herself. She didn't care how different the environment was, what problems she'd have to cope with. Her strong sense of self-worth demanded she make good on her own abilities...not by being a playboy's mistress!

She opened the book on her lap, determined on focusing her mind on the future. A map on the first page showed the Kimberly region—three hundred and twenty thousand square kilometres, stretching from the seaport of Broome on the high west coast of Australia to the border of the Northern Territory. Blocked out in green was King's Eden—a big chunk of outback country that would be the last place on earth Bobby Hewson would look for her.

It might not be the Garden of Eden, but at least it had no serpent in it. With that blessed assurance in her mind, Miranda turned the page and began reading, acutely aware of having turned a page in her life and there was only one way to go...forward.

CHAPTER TWO

"JUST tell me one thing, Mother. Why choose a woman?"

Because you need one.

And with Susan Butler finally out of your life, you might look for more than a convenient mistress.

Elizabeth King hid these thoughts as she assessed the depth of her eldest son's annoyance at the decision she'd made. The irritable note in his voice and the V creased between his brows, plus the tense impatience of his actions since he'd entered the sitting-room, did not promise an encouraging start between Nathan and Miranda Wade, whom he was about to meet.

Running the resort was part of Tommy's business. Running the cattle station was his, and he drew a firm line between the two enterprises. For the most part, Nathan kept his world to himself, but to Elizabeth's mind, that had to change.

He was thirty-five years old. Time for him to get married. Time for him to have children. Passing that particular buck to his younger brothers wouldn't wash. It was Nathan who had inherited the major share of Lachlan's genes and Elizabeth didn't want to see them wasted.

"I chose the person with the best qualifications to manage the resort," she answered, raising a quizzical eyebrow at the man who was so very much his father's son. "I wasn't aware you held any prejudice against women taking on responsible positions, Nathan."

He threw her a mocking look from the leather armchair he'd made his, since it was the only one big enough to accommodate his length and breadth comfortably. "Not even you could stick it out here all year around."

That old argument wouldn't wash, either. "I had other interests to look after, as you very well know."

His eyes remained sceptical. "The point is, we all agreed a married couple was the best choice."

"Fine, if the marriage is stable," Elizabeth retorted, a pointed reminder that the last manager had left under threat of divorce by his wife. "And who is to judge how good a relationship is, on an interview where everyone puts their best foot forward? We've been down that track."

"Then I would have thought a single man would cope with the location better than a single woman," he argued.

Elizabeth shrugged. "I wasn't impressed with the men who applied. A bit too soft for my liking."

"So what have we got? A woman of steel?" His mouth thinned. "She'd better be, because I will not be at her beck and call to clean up any mess she makes of it. If she needs someone to hold her hand, Tommy can do it."

"I'm sure you can make that clear to her, Nathan." Elizabeth could not repress a satisfied little smile as she added, "If you wish to."

Nathan's black eyebrows beetled down. "What's that supposed to mean?"

"I doubt Miranda Wade would be inclined to cling to any man's hand." *And that, my son, may well set a sexual challenge you'll find hard to resist.*

"Just what we need—a raging feminist to play charming hostess to the resort guests who expect to be pampered," he commented derisively.

"Oh, I think someone who's been in the hospitality trade for twelve years knows how to manage guests," Elizabeth drawled. "But judge for yourself, Nathan. That sounds like Tommy's vehicle arriving now. I trust you'll make an effort to be welcoming."

He rolled his eyes and muttered, "I'm sure Tommy will be in good form. He'll undoubtedly cover any lapse on my part."

True, Elizabeth thought. Her highly extroverted middle son was probably flirting his head off with Miranda Wade right now. It was second nature to Tommy to spark a response in women. He liked to be liked. But the cool blonde she'd interviewed would let his charm wash over her like water off a duck's back. Those green eyes of hers had burned with a need to prove something to herself. They were focused inwardly, not outwardly.

It would be interesting to see if Nathan drew a flicker of awareness from her, Nathan who was what he was and you could like him or not as you pleased. He was a challenge, too. A challenge most women gave up on. Elizabeth didn't think Miranda Wade was the giving-up type. Even so, the equation still needed the right chemistry, and no one could make that happen.

Such a capricious element—sexual chemistry—but vital. She could only hope…

Miranda had seen it from the air this morning—the area comprising the resort and the layout of the cattle station. She hadn't realised the buildings relating to each business would be entirely separate, the "homestead" at the resort having no connection whatsoever to the family homestead. The former was of very modern design and construction. The latter, as it was approached at ground level, gathered an allure that touched an empty place in her life.

Deep roots had been put down here, the kind of roots she had never known. Nothing had been fixed or solid in her mother's life and Miranda had been glad to get out of it, knowing she was an unwelcome reminder of her mother's mistake, a reminder of her age, too, as well as a resented distraction to the men who'd kept her.

As soon as she was sixteen, she'd left and had been in live-in hotel positions ever since, not really letting her surroundings touch her. They were simply places that put a roof over her head. She had no sense of *home*, no sense of family tradition, no sense of belonging to anything except herself.

It felt strange, coming face-to-face with something so different to her own experience. No modern landscaping here. The trees that had been planted for both shade and ornament were old, the girth of their trunks and the breadth of their branches proclaiming the growth of more years than any one person's lifetime. The intense entanglement of the multicoloured bougainvillea hedge surrounding the house indicated longevity, as well.

Like all the buildings on the cattle station, the homestead was white, set off by an expanse of green lawns. However, it sat alone, on a rise above the river, and the verandahs with their ornamentation of cast-iron balustrading and frieze panels, topped by the symmetrical peaks of its roof gave it the appearance of a shining crown on top of all the land it overlooked.

As Tommy King drove his Jeep up to the front steps, she was prompted by the sheer scale of the house to ask, "When was this built?"

"Oh, coming up ninety years ago," he answered with one of his sparkling grins. "One of the first King brothers here—Gerald it was—saw some government official's home in Queensland and was so impressed with it, he copied the design and had all the materials shipped to Wyndham."

Cost no object, Miranda thought, recalling from the book she'd read that the first pioneering King brothers had mined a fortune in gold at Kalgoorlie before taking up this land.

"It's very impressive," she murmured, thinking houses simply weren't built to such huge proportions any more. Certainly not in suburbia, she amended, smiling ruefully at her limited knowledge.

"It used to serve many purposes in the old days," Tommy cheerfully explained. "Everyone lived in and travellers passing through stopped by for days to rest up. Hospitality has always been big in the outback."

"I guess it broke the sense of isolation," Miranda remarked.

"Well, taking to the air fixes that now," he answered, his handsome face beaming pleasure in the accessibility he provided.

She'd learnt he owned and ran an airline company from Kununurra, small plane and helicopter charters making up the bulk of his business, much of which was connected to the resort. Tommy King was a go-getter entrepreneur, with the confidence, likeable personality and gift of the gab that could sell anything. Most of all himself.

Miranda wasn't about to buy. The charm came too easily, and while he might be a shrewd businessman and definitely no lightweight for a man only in his early thirties, he had playboy looks; a riot of black curly hair that bobbed endearingly over his forehead, dark dancing eyes inviting flirtatious fun, a face as handsome as sin, and a lean, athletic body exuding charismatic energy and sex appeal.

She'd been in his company since he'd collected her from Kununurra airport this morning and as an informative guide he was excellent, but she was determined on keeping a very firm personal distance between them. The likes of Tommy King could not tempt her into mixing business with pleasure. She hoped he was getting that message because she certainly didn't want an awkward situation developing between them.

"This place is getting to be like a white elephant now," he commented as he brought the Jeep to a halt. "Wasted..." He shook his head over the wicked shame of it. "Guests would probably give their eye-teeth to stay here, but Nathan just won't hear of it." He grimaced, though his dark eyes twinkled cheerfully at her as he added, "Like a brick wall, my brother."

Nathan...oldest son of Elizabeth and Lachlan. Just as well she had studied the family tree in the book on

King's Eden. The people she'd met so far assumed she knew these details about the Kings as well as they did.

"It's understandable that he prefers privacy for his family," Miranda said, thinking some things came ahead of turning everything into dollars.

"If he ever got himself married and had a family, I'd agree," Tommy shot back at her. "As it is, he's here by himself most of the time, and that doesn't look like changing."

He alighted from the Jeep, quickly striding around it to open Miranda's door for her. She had little time to digest this new information. The invitation to dine with the family at the old homestead tonight had seemed to encompass more than the actual reality of one man. Two, counting Tommy.

"I thought Mrs King lived here, too," she said as she stepped out of the Jeep.

"Not on any regular basis. Mum's fairly tied up in Broome, managing the pearl farm…"

Pearls…

He grinned. "…but she flew in yesterday to be on hand to greet you and make sure everything is to your satisfaction."

Her inner tension eased. She wouldn't be the only woman at the dinner table. Elizabeth King would undoubtedly direct the conversation tonight and provide a comfort zone. Miranda smiled. "How kind of her!"

Tommy laughed. "Mum is a diplomat from way back."

They proceeded up the steps, Miranda wondering just how different the two brothers were and how much their mother had to work at welding their separate interests into a reasonably harmonious unit. "Isn't there a third son?" she asked tentatively, her mind seeing three names listed in print—Nathan, Thomas, Jared.

But the book on King's Eden had been written some years ago. She had assumed marriages would have taken place since then. Having been wrong on that score with Tommy and Nathan, and with no mention being made of a younger brother from Tommy, she wondered if something had happened to the third son.

"Oh, Jared flits around the mining operations and oversees what's done with the pearls. He's hardly ever here," came the offhand reply. "You'll probably meet him some time or other but not tonight. I think he's in Hong Kong at the moment."

Mining operations...

Miranda did a very quick mental readjustment about the King family. What she was meeting here was very serious wealth, on a similar scale, if not higher, than the Hewson family. All three of the King brothers would be used to getting what they wanted, just as Bobby was. When they married, it would undoubtedly be into a family who had connections to their business interests and could probably broaden and enhance them. That was the way their kind of world worked.

She was an outsider, an employee who had her uses. Miranda resolved to keep those *uses* strictly defined. No blurred lines. However attractive any of the King men were, they were out of bounds in any personal sense.

She would never allow herself to be flattered by Tommy's show of interest. If Nathan had a brick wall around him, it could stay totally intact, as far as she was concerned. Jared was more or less out of the picture so she didn't have the problem of proximity with him.

Best to concentrate completely on Elizabeth King tonight.

With this decision firmly settled in her mind, Miranda's attention turned to observing features of the house she was entering. Leadlight windows surrounded the solid cedar door Tommy opened for her. As she stepped into the main entrance hall, she realised it ran right through to the back of the house and actually formed a gallery of framed photographs. A collection of King's Eden history, she wondered, but didn't have the opportunity to look.

Tommy walked straight to the first door off the hallway and ushered her into a sitting room so full of riches, she was momentarily dazed by all there was to see. Much of the decor had an Asian influence, yet there seemed be an eclectic range of styles that somehow melded together into a fascinating collection.

Her skating gaze was halted—joltingly—by the man rising from a large leather armchair, a man whose length seemed to climb up like a mountain, blocking everything else out. He had to be well over six foot, broad-shouldered, broad-chested, one of the biggest men Miranda had ever met, and all of him emitting hard muscular strength that gave way to nothing.

Unaccountably a convulsive little shiver ran down her spine. His sheer physical presence had an impact that seemed to hit her whole nervous system, leaving her with an odd tremulous feeling that was deeply disturbing. He wasn't threatening her. He stood out of courtesy. She had no cause to feel...vulnerable.

With a sense of self-determination, Miranda made eye contact with him and plastered a polite little smile on her face. *His* face could have been carved out of brown granite—all hard, sharp planes. Even the curves of his mouth seemed carved, defined emphatically, as though to deny any softness. Absolutely nothing "pretty-playboy" about Nathan King.

His thick black hair was straight. His black brows were straight. And cutting straight across the room at her were laser-sharp blue eyes, the vivid intensity of their colour made all the more stunning by his darkly tanned skin. Miranda felt utterly pinned by them, unable to break their captivating power...until Elizabeth King spoke.

"Welcome to King's Eden..."

Miranda jerked her head towards the distinctive, familiar voice. The woman who had hired her sat on an ornately carved armchair, its rich scarlet and gold silk upholstery forming a striking frame for her white hair and white pantsuit. And the beautiful pearls around her neck.

"It's both a pleasure and a privilege to be here, Mrs King," Miranda managed to reply with creditable aplomb. "Thank you for inviting me."

The older woman was smiling, her dark eyes warm with some private satisfaction. She waved attention back to her son. "This is Nathan, who has the controlling hand on the station. Miranda Wade, Nathan, our new resort manager."

He remained precisely where he was, sizing her up,

silent, formidable, daunting, challenging. For a moment, Miranda remained pinned, but the long years of training for greeting people urged her forward. Taking the initiative always broke the ice. She had to associate with this man, when business required his co-operation. Some kind of reasonable footing with him had to be developed.

Yet all the stern reasoning in her mind had no strengthening effect on her legs. They were alarmingly shaky as she stepped forward to offer her hand to Nathan King. This was a man who would dominate everything he touched...and she was about to touch him.

CHAPTER THREE

NATHAN was stunned. He'd seen many beautiful women but none quite as striking as this one. From head to foot she was something else...built on a scale that accentuated every womanly asset. And she certainly had them all!

She almost matched Tommy in height, which had to put her close to six feet tall and she wasn't wearing high heels. Her hair was an instant tactile temptation, a softly curved fall to her shoulders, gleaming with a fascinating blend of blonde shades from silver to strawberry.

The classical perfection of her face was made even more intriguing by the slight cleft at the centre of her chinline, and the long neck below it promised an alluring suppleness. Her honey-gold skin glowed—face, arms, legs—all bare, and her limbs were as perfectly proportioned as her face.

She wore a rather high-necked, sleeveless dress that skimmed her lushly curved figure, the skirt flaring to just above her knees, a modest dress but boldly coloured in an abstract floral pattern on black. Splotches of lemon, orange, lime green, turquoise, royal blue seemed to leap off the black background, a dazzling kaleidoscope of colour. On her feet were strappy lemon sandals.

A very confident woman, Nathan thought, prepared

to stand out rather than blend in. A strong individual. Certainly no shy violet or clinging vine. A long dormant excitement began to stir in him. This might be a woman worth knowing...an experience worth having.

The visual pleasure of her was too enticing to give up. He stayed where he stood, letting her move forward to formalise his mother's introduction. Lovely, almond-shaped, green eyes, as uniquely distinctive as the rest of her. Honey-brown lashes and brows. Was the hair-colour natural?

"I'm delighted to meet you, Mr King," she said with cool deliberation as she held out her hand.

Establishing impersonal distance.

Nathan barely stopped himself from grinning at the implicit challenge as he gripped her hand, enfolding it in his own, liking the soft, silky warmth of it. His smile was controlled into a mere expression of friendly acknowledgement. Playing the stand-offish game suited him just as well, while he took her measure.

"Even the children on the station call me Nathan, so please feel comfortable with it," he assured her. "And since the resort also operates on a first name basis, I trust I may call you Miranda."

"Of course," she answered smoothly, starting to extract her hand.

Nathan did not resist the movement, finding it interesting she felt the need to break the physical link with him so quickly. It wasn't exactly a rude rejection of contact, more a discomfort with it. Did she sense what she was stirring in him? Was she stirred herself? Her eyes reflected no more than the obliging interest of an employee to an employer, not so much as a hint of speculation on a woman to man basis.

His mother's words came back to him... *I doubt Miranda Wade would be inclined to cling to any man's hand.*

"What would you like to drink?" he asked, wondering if she was a raging feminist. "My mother's having champagne..."

"A glass of water would be fine," she quickly interposed.

Keeping a cool head, Nathan thought as he nodded and disconnected himself from her by turning to his brother. "A beer for you, Tommy?"

"Thanks, Nathan," came the ready agreement.

He left them to sort out seating while he got the drinks from the bar in the adjoining billiard room. Miranda Wade was not a woman to be rushed. That much was obvious. He had the impression there were many layers to her, not an easy woman to tag in any sense.

He wondered how Tommy was faring with her. His brother had spent most of the day in her company. Had he managed to draw any sparks of interest? Resolving to simply sit and watch the interplay between them, Nathan returned with the drinks, ironically amused at the way this meeting was turning out. His annoyance with his mother's decision had winked out the moment Miranda Wade had appeared in person.

She'd chosen to sit in an armchair close to his mother, right across the room from where he'd been seated. Tommy bridged the gap, having dropped onto a sofa that could have invited sharing, but that option had not been taken up by the fair Miranda. She nodded to a drink coaster on the small table beside her as Nathan approached and gave him a flashing smile of acknowledgement when he set the glass down where she'd indicated.

"Thank you," she said, breaking briefly from her conversation with his mother, then instantly resuming it.

Done with grace, but holding him at a very firm distance, Nathan observed. He didn't linger, didn't attempt to draw her attention. A two-year contract gave him plenty of time to make her acquaintance. He strolled over to Tommy and handed him the beer.

"Happy with the choice?" he asked quietly, watching for any reservation in his brother's expressive eyes.

"Are you?" Tommy retorted, mischief dancing.

Nathan shrugged. "Your business, Tommy."

"An asset, I think." Definitely male appreciation in the gaze he slanted at Miranda. However his mouth made a wry little moue as he added, "Mind very focused on the job."

"Glad to hear it," Nathan murmured and moved back to his chair, content with the confirmation that his brother's charm had failed to evoke the usual response.

This now promised to be a most interesting evening. Didn't feminists preach wanting men, not needing them? Sexual freedom? Taking as they pleased? What if Miranda Wade wanted what he wanted?

Miranda was grateful the meal had been easy to eat—prawns cooked with coconut and served with a mango sauce, followed by barramundi, and now a melt-in-the-mouth passion-fruit mousse. Dining with the Kings was certainly a testing experience, but she thought she'd managed the evening reasonably well, given the unnerving presence of the man at the head of the table.

Nathan had barely said a word during the dinner conversation, but she was acutely aware of him listening to everything she said, the turn of his head towards her, the silent force of his concentrated attention. She sensed he was cataloguing her questions, her responses, her opinions, building up a picture of the kind of person she was while giving nothing of himself away.

The worst of it was, she kept remembering how his hand had felt, wrapped around hers. Maybe it was because he was the cattle King, but the impression he had left was one of branding her with his imprint. She wished he wasn't quite so big, so overwhelmingly *male*. It made her ridiculously conscious of being female, disconcertingly so since not even Bobby Hewson had triggered such a disturbingly pervasive effect on her.

Fortunately, both Tommy, sitting across the table from her, and Elizabeth King at the foot of it, had been very relaxed in their manner towards her, friendly, helpful, informative. And the dining room itself was a fascinating distraction from the man who dominated too much of it.

All the furniture here was of beautiful, polished mahogany. China cabinets held a magnificent array of treasures. The paintings on the walls were of birds and executed in splendid detail. Everything looked in mint condition and Miranda wondered about the household staff. Dinner had been served by a middle-aged woman, introduced as Nancy, but there had to be several people looking after this amazing place.

Elizabeth King casually remarked, "I think it would be a good idea for Miranda to do the regular tourist trips before the season really gets underway at the resort. She should know at firsthand what she's recommending to guests."

Tommy frowned. "Sam's still laid up with a sprained ankle…"

Miranda had already met Samantha Connelly, the resident helicopter pilot at the resort, a generally pleasant young woman, though bluntly terse in response to Tommy's teasing over her temporary handicap.

"I'm flying down to the Bungle Bungle Range, day after tomorrow. Miranda can come with me if she likes."

The words were spoken offhandedly, yet coming so unexpectedly from Nathan, they had the effect of a thunderbolt cracking through the air, jolting the rest of the company.

Tommy's head swivelled towards his older brother. *"You?"*

The astonishment in his voice heightened the weird panic attacking Miranda's stomach. She had to force herself to glance at the man who was offering her his company on a one-to-one basis. It felt as though her whole body was screaming danger. Yet there was nothing on his face to indicate any special interest in her.

He raised an eyebrow at Tommy as though his brother was over-reacting to a perfectly natural suggestion. "Some problem?" he asked.

"And never the twain shall meet except during the

June muster,'' Tommy drily taunted. ''Here it is only
March, Nathan, and you're offering to help with resort
business?''

''Hardly business,'' he retorted just as drily. ''I'm
making the trip anyway. It's an opportunity going begging if Miranda wants to take it up.''

His gaze swung to her inquiringly.

Trapped in a small plane or helicopter with *him?* Her
mind scurried to find some excuse not to accept.

''What are you going for?'' Tommy asked, giving
her more time.

The mesmerising blue eyes released her as they targeted his brother again. ''The head park ranger wants
to borrow the Sarah King diaries on the local
Aboriginal tribes. Background reading. I said I'd drop
them in to him.''

''Well, that fixes one trip for you, Miranda,''
Elizabeth King said brightly, her face beaming satisfaction.

''But, Mrs King, the day after tomorrow...''
Miranda frowned. ''I see this week as very busy, getting myself familiarised with the workings of the resort
and checking the intake of staff for the season. Much
as I appreciate the offer, Nathan—'' she quickly con-
structed a look of apologetic appeal ''—I have barely
arrived and...''

''Best to go while you can, Miranda,'' Elizabeth
King interjected firmly. ''Besides, it won't be taking
up Samantha's time or using one of Tommy's pilots.
This is much the more economical arrangement.''

Which neatly whipped the mat out from under

Miranda's feet, since insistence on some other time would cost the resort money.

"A dawn trip, Nathan?" his mother went on, having dispensed with any further protest from Miranda.

"Oh, I daresay we can catch the sunrise," he answered.

Miranda sat seething as they settled the arrangements between them, totally ignoring whether what was being decided suited her or not. The arrogance of wealth, she thought, moving people around like pawns to their will. She barely quelled the urge to make a stand against them. The problem was she wasn't familiar with the outback and firsthand experience of it probably was important in handling her job well.

And, in fact, she wouldn't be objecting at all if it wasn't Nathan she had to accompany. He rattled her. She didn't feel in control with him. *Get a grip on yourself, Miranda,* she sternly berated herself. Like it or not, she had to deal with Nathan King, and maybe getting to know him better was the best way. He might lose his attraction on closer acquaintance.

"I'll have you back at the resort by noon," he assured her.

Six hours close to him. "Thank you," she said, her heart fluttering in agitation.

"What do you think of it?"

"Pardon?" What was he referring to?

His eyes glinted with amused mockery, making her even more nervous. Did he sense how she felt about him?

"The resort. Since you've always held a city position, I wondered how it looked to you. I presume Tommy took you on a tour of it this afternoon.''

"The accommodation sectors are exceptionally well planned," she could answer with confidence. "The homestead is brilliantly located, and the decor very attractive. Everything looks top class.''

One eyebrow rose challengingly. "No sinking heart feeling? No uneasy twang of, What have I done?''

She laughed and shook her head. "More, How marvellous! I'm really looking forward to taking over and making the best of it.''

"A new world for you.''

"Yes.''

"Most people hang onto the world they know.''

"I guess I'm not most people.''

"An adventuress? Looking for something different?''

"More satisfying a need for something different.''

"Then I hope all your needs are satisfied here.''

"That would indeed be Eden.''

He laughed, his whole face springing alive so strikingly, Miranda was totally captivated by it. Her mind was zinging from the quick repartee between them and her body was pumping adrenaline so fast, every part of her felt highly invigorated.

His eyes literally danced with pleasure, shooting tingles of it into her bloodstream as he remarked, "I tend to think Eden is what we fashion for ourselves. It seems to me that's what our choices are about…aiming for what will give us a happy situation.''

She was suddenly hit by a shockwave of intimacy that had to be turned back. Common sense insisted on ringing down a warning that life wasn't quite as easy as that. "Unfortunately we can't control the choices other people make," she replied, her eyes trying to cool the warmth in his. "And that can create a hell for us."

"You can always walk away."

"But will they respect that?"

"Make them."

"I'm not quite as big as you, Nathan," she retorted lightly.

He smiled. "But you do have a mind of your own, Miranda. And very interesting it is."

"Thank you."

"Oh, I should be thanking you. I'm sure you will take any boredom out of our trip together."

Miranda's breath caught in her throat. He didn't mean the flight to the Bungle Bungle Range. She knew he didn't. He meant the continuing journey of a close acquaintance spreading over the two years she was going to be here. And that was going to be very, very dangerous to any peace of mind.

"Well, don't forget to be a tour guide, as well, Nathan," Tommy drawled. "This is resort business."

Was there a touch of resentment in his voice. A flash of sibling rivalry? Miranda quickly switched her attention to the man whose interests she would be looking after. "I'll make the most of the trip, Tommy," she assured him. "I know how essential it is that I do." *She mustn't—not for one moment—forget her place.*

He nodded.

"I'm sure you'll find it an amazing experience," Elizabeth King put in with an approving smile.

Miranda hoped so. She would need every amazing distraction she could get to keep holding Nathan King at a distance.

CHAPTER FOUR

NEEDING to push Nathan King out of her mind and
gain a sense of control over her immediate environment, Miranda filled her first morning at King's Eden
with a staff meeting. Since the resort was only open
from the beginning of April to the end of November,
the full complement of employees was not yet in res-
idence, but the maintenance crew and those in charge
of each accommodation level and amenities rolled up
to meet and assess their new manager.

Miranda was very aware of not having the firsthand
knowledge of this area, while those facing her did.
She'd had no experience of the Big Wet, the mon-
soonal rains that made much of the Top End of
Australia inaccessible by road during the summer
months, but the oppressive heat outside was enough to
convince her the December to March period was not a
good time to travel to this part of the outback for sight-
seeing, even by air. She blessed the fact the resort
homestead was air-conditioned, or she'd be wilting in
front of these people.

They had spread themselves around the large living
area, which had been designed for the pleasure and
comfort of top-paying guests. The slate floor in blue-
green hues looked invitingly cool and the cane furniture with its brightly patterned cushions lent a relaxing,
tropical feel to the room. Aboriginal artefacts and

paintings were reminders of how close visitors were to an ancient heritage. A wall of glass gave a view of the resort pool and some of the outdoors chairs had been brought inside to accommodate everyone.

Miranda had deliberately chosen this normally exclusive leisure room as the gathering place, wanting to set the tone of a top team getting together. The resort restaurant was used for staff meetings when business was in full swing, but this was only the key group who would be answering directly to her and she needed to get them onside.

They all wore casual clothes, shorts and T-shirts, a different vision of staff for her, accustomed as she was to more formal uniforms. Miranda had donned a lime-green sleeveless shift, wanting the effect of both dignity and simplicity, and she'd wound her hair up for a look of neat efficiency, but she quickly decided that tailored safari shorts and shirt were more the style for this resort. Stupid to look out of place.

Apart from a couple of men on the maintenance crew, everyone else was younger than she was, very young in terms of managerial positions. Understandable in such a location, she quickly reasoned. A spirit of adventure had probably brought them here, wanting the outback experience while they were still footloose and fancy free, or at least not tied down with families.

She spent most of the meeting asking questions, listening to reports, inviting suggestions for resolving problems, which were raised, keeping discussions open while she absorbed the easy camaraderie amongst the staff and made notes on the practicalities of getting things done in time for the beginning of the season.

Over and over again, mention was made of problems caused by cancelling the regular time-off for the transient service staff. They went stir-crazy, becoming careless and rude to guests. Breaks away from the isolation of the resort restored their good humour. It only raised trouble if too many bookings required the postponing of leave.

Miranda took on board that everyone was keen for her to understand this. Isolation was a very real social problem. Her mind drifted to the King family…a hundred years of living in isolation…Nathan running the cattle station…alone, unmarried. Did he ever feel stir-crazy? Would she, here at King's Eden?

Paradise or hell?

Too late to change her decision to take this job on, Miranda sternly reminded herself. Whatever its difficulties, she *would* see it through. Nathan had been subtly challenging her on that last night. Her jaw tightened as she recalled his amused mockery. She would show him!

Having collected all the information she wanted from her staff, Miranda brought the meeting to a close with a personal policy statement, emphasising that good hospitality depended on good communication and she didn't want any breakdowns in that area. Anticipation of guest requirements was her other main point and she would be instituting checks that would help to ensure this.

The response was nods and smiles of satisfaction. Having memorised names throughout the morning,

Miranda made a point of using them as the dispersing staff made friendly parting comments. Samantha Connelly, the injured helicopter pilot, stayed behind, her sprained ankle propped on a footstool.

"Do you need help?" Miranda asked with a sympathetic smile.

"I'm here to help you," was the dry reply. "Until I can throw away these wretched crutches."

She leaned over the side of the armchair to pick up the resented aids to her disability. Sensing a fierce independence Miranda made no move to do it for her. She admired the head of burnished copper curls as it bobbed down and noticed the well-defined musculature in the young woman's arms. Samantha Connelly was built on a smaller and more slender scale than Miranda herself, but she was certainly lithe and strong.

"I hate being hobbled," she muttered as her face came up, though her expression was one of wry resignation as she added, "Stuck in an office instead of flying high."

"I didn't realise you did office work, as well," Miranda said in surprise.

"Oh, I fill in, taking the resort bookings at the Kununurra Headquarters during the Wet. Not so much charter business then. I've loaded all the facts and figures into your computer here, so if you need a hand with anything until your clerical assistant clocks on…"

"I'd appreciate it," Miranda said warmly.

"No problem." Samantha slid her leg off the footstool and heaved herself out of the armchair.

Miranda had the impression of a pride that would always deny personal problems and minimise others as much as possible. The young pilot had a rather narrow, gamine face, her fair skin liberally freckled, yet an innate strength of character seemed to shine through its finely boned structure and her sky-blue eyes would undoubtedly scorn any suggestion of cuteness.

"How did you get into flying?" Miranda asked, as they set off towards the wide hallway that bisected the homestead and led to the administration and accommodation wings.

"I was born to it," came the dismissive reply. "Since I'm currently grounded, I guess Tommy jumped in and offered to fly you around the regular tours." She slanted Miranda a derisive look. "Only too eager to show you the sights, I'll bet."

Caution was instantly pricked. "Why should he be eager, Samantha?"

"Call me Sam. Everyone else does." Another derisive look. "And if you didn't notice Tommy's tongue hanging out yesterday, I sure did. To put it bluntly, Miranda, you're stacked in all the right places and gorgeous to boot. So don't tell me he didn't give you the rush."

Jealousy? The acid little thread in Sam's tone alerted Miranda to very sensitive ground here. "Well, I guess the rush got diverted," she answered dryly. "In any event I'm not interested in a personal relationship with Tommy King."

"You're not?" Sam stopped, eyeing Miranda with sheer astonishment. "Most women fall for him like ninepins."

She shrugged. "You can chalk up a miss as far as I'm concerned."

A gleeful grin lit up Sam's face. "I've never known Tommy strike out. What a lovely dent in his ego!"

"Do you know him very well?"

"Too well." The grin turned into a grimace. "Like I'm the kid sister he never had. I've been working for the Kings for years, mustering cattle, even before the resort was built."

Which explained the familiarity between Sam and Tommy, the teasing and her disrespectful responses yesterday. "Then you must know Nathan well, too." The words slipped out before Miranda could bite on her tongue. She didn't want to reveal any curiosity about him. She didn't even want to think about him.

"I know all of them well," Sam replied with feeling, sounding exasperated by them or their family attitudes.

She set off down the hall again and Miranda kept pace with her, grateful the subject was apparently dropped.

"Come to think of it," Sam muttered. "It's not like Tommy to give up." She frowned at Miranda. "Didn't he even line up one trip with you?"

Miranda stifled a sigh. No point in hiding what would soon be common knowledge. "Nathan is flying me to the Bungle Bungle Range tomorrow," she stated flatly.

"Nathan?" Another dead halt as Sam stared wide-eyed at her. "Nathan's taking you?"

"He's going anyway," Miranda explained, trying to keep a terse note out of her voice. "He plans to take some old diaries about the Aboriginal tribes to the park ranger there."

Sam's mouth twitched. Her eyes danced with inner hilarity. "Nothing to do with you, of course."

"Just a ready opportunity," Miranda said dismissively.

Sam laughed out loud. "Oh, I wish I could have seen Tommy's face when Nathan beat him to the draw."

She chuckled on and off, little bursts of private amusement, all the way to the main administration office. Miranda hid her vexation behind silence, disdaining any comment, yet the memory of Tommy's face at the dinner table last night kept playing through her mind.

She hoped the two King brothers were not going to make her the meat in their sandwich. Would they respect her choice not to get personally involved with either of them? It could become very unpleasant if they didn't.

Miranda's stomach was churning by the time she and Sam finally settled in the office, both of them in chairs, facing the computer on her desk. She needed to get her thoughts focused on business again. Tomorrow morning she would face what she had to with Nathan King. Until then…

"He's free," Sam said with a sidelong look at her.

"I beg your pardon?" Miranda answered distractedly, watching the monitor screen as the computer went through its start procedure.

"Nathan…he's unattached right now. The woman he was seeing got married. He hasn't started up with anyone else yet."

"Well, I guess he's feeling rejected," Miranda commented, hoping she sounded careless, though she was amazed that Nathan King had been turned down for some other man.

"Oh, she didn't reject him. It wasn't that kind of relationship. Just casual lovers, really, though it did go on for a few years."

Miranda gritted her teeth as anger blazed through her. *Casual lovers!* More like a convenient mistress who finally wised up and got herself a man who really loved her. If Nathan King was harbouring the idea that *she* could now fall into that convenient slot, he could think again. One way or another she would make her position very clear to him tomorrow.

"Shall we get down to business?" she said coldly, drawing a startled glance from Sam.

"Sure! Just thought you might like to know about Nathan."

"I know all I need to know, Sam. He's a member of the King family. Okay?"

Wide blue eyes met green ice and curiosity was instantly quenched. "Fine!" Sam's gaze snapped to the monitor screen. "The bookings are listed in time sequence and..."

Finally...business!

Miranda savagely recalled Tommy King saying Nathan was a brick wall. She vowed that the cattle King would meet a steel wall tomorrow, with barbed wire on top to deter any attempt at scaling it.

CHAPTER FIVE

MIRANDA was already at the resort helipad when Nathan pulled up in his Jeep. She had arrived five minutes before the arranged time of meeting, driving one of the luggage buggies, which she'd commandeered for her use. Being early made her feel more prepared, more on top of the situation.

Even so, Nathan swung himself out of the Jeep and Miranda's breath caught in her throat. Regardless of her mental shields, his physical impact got to her, a big blast of strong maleness that instantly set everything female in her aquiver. Like herself, he was dressed in shorts, shirt, walking boots, a hat in one hand, a backpack dangling from his shoulder, but he emanated purposeful vitality while she felt hopelessly paralysed.

"Good morning," he said, shooting a smile at her that jump-started her heart again. "We've struck it lucky with a cloudless sky. A clear sunrise makes the colours more vivid."

"Yes, it is a good morning," she agreed, though it promised a hot, hot day to come. In more ways than one, given her instinctive response to him.

He waved her towards the helicopter on the pad and she fell into step beside him, concentrating on injecting more steel into her spine.

"Have you read anything about the Bungle Bungle Range?" he asked.

"Only what was in the tour pamphlet."

"Well, seeing says it all."

Clearly he was not interested in lecturing or showing off his local knowledge, but his interest in her was twinkling from his eyes and playing havoc with Miranda's nerves.

"Having trouble sleeping?" he asked.

"No," she instantly denied, wondering if she looked tired from last night's tossing and turning over this meeting. "Why should I?" she challenged, wanting to pin-point the reason for his speculation.

"Oh, the quiet sometimes gets to city people. They miss the background noise, and other things they're used to."

Like sex?

Miranda found her jaw clenching and mentally berated herself for being ultra-sensitive. On the surface his comment was perfectly reasonable. On the surface he wasn't saying or doing anything she could take objection to. But under the surface she felt the buzz of possibilities that were far from innocent.

"The last two days have been so busy, I guess the quiet hasn't impressed itself on me yet," she answered.

"It will," he said matter-of-factly. "You'll come to like it or hate it. One thing can be said definitively about the outback. It very quickly sorts out the visitors and the stayers."

"So I understand. I've been told there can be a stir-crazy problem with some of the staff if they don't get regular leave." That moved the conversation to a more impersonal level!

"Not just with staff," he returned drily. "Most women I've known."

He slanted her a look that seemed to be weighing if she had the grit to be a stayer. It set Miranda wondering about the woman who'd chosen to marry someone else...a woman who didn't want to spend her life on a cattle station? But why would Nathan King keep the relationship going for years if it hadn't suited him?

"There must be women who were born and bred to the outback like you," she said pertinently. "Like Sam Connelly."

"Ah, Sam," he said in a tone of fond indulgence. He slid her an ironic look. "There aren't many like Sam, believe me, and she only has eyes for Tommy. One of these days he might stop chasing glitter and see the gold right under his nose."

Was that true about Sam? Miranda tucked the information away for future reference and targeted the man who was criticising his brother. "Perhaps he's not inclined to look. Some men don't want real commitment to a woman."

"Is that personal experience speaking?"

Bitterly personal. Miranda barely stemmed a burning rush of blood as she fought those memories, determined not to reveal her humiliation to a man who'd spent two years pleasuring himself with a woman he must have considered *unsuitable* for marriage. Why else would he have let her go to another man? With cool deliberation Miranda turned the question back on him.

"I was just wondering why *you* haven't found gold somewhere in this vast Kimberly region."

His mouth quirked, drawing her attention to its sensual promise. "Funny thing about gold. It has certain chemical properties. If they're missing it's just fool's gold."

"Maybe they're missing for Tommy," she argued, all too aware of the chemistry Nathan tapped in her.

"No. He covers it with teasing. Sam covers it with aggression. And Tommy's damned fool ego gets in the way. He'd add you to his pride list if he could."

They'd crossed the ground to the helicopter. Nathan opened the door for her. Miranda didn't immediately step up to the passenger seat. She stood stockstill, her mind whirling back over her evening with the Kings...Nathan, stand-offish, watching, only inserting himself when Tommy was considering taking her on tour trips. Had she got Nathan's purpose with her entirely wrong? Nothing to do with sexual attraction?

She eyed him directly. "Is this what today is about, Nathan? Putting yourself between me and Tommy to save Sam's feelings?"

He returned a look that simmered with appreciative warmth, liking her bluntness. "From what I observed, you're not particularly drawn to him, Miranda. But Tommy doesn't give up easily..."

Sam's words!

"...and as time goes on, you might find yourself getting bored enough to play with his interest. Proximity and availability tend to overcome other shortcomings."

"I see. You're warning me off."

"No. It's your choice. I don't believe in interfering with people's choices. I'd be sorry to see Sam hurt, though. It's one thing knowing Tommy drifts in and out of affairs, quite another watching one at close quarters.''

''I take your point,'' she conceded, knowing she wasn't interested in getting involved with Tommy King anyway.

Nathan nodded, then suddenly grinned at her, his blue eyes dancing with more than appreciation. ''Besides, I'd much prefer you to relieve your boredom with me.''

''What?'' Her mouth fell open and stayed open in surprise at the abrupt switch from do-gooding friend of Sam to man making a move on her.

Miranda barely had time to register his words, let alone his intent as he stepped closer, cupped her cheek, tilted her chin, and with his eyes blazing into hers, wickedly inviting, teasing, wanting, he murmured, ''Let's try it, shall we?''

Then he was *kissing* her, soft, seductive pressures that kept her shocked in stillness. She hadn't been expecting it, wasn't prepared for it, and his very gentleness was both confusing and tantalising. It was a take, but there was nothing really offensive about...about the way his mouth was loving hers. Yet he really had no right to just do it like this. She should stop it. Where would it lead? Where *could* it lead?

She lifted her hands. They clamped onto his chest, but instead of pushing, they found a magnetic attraction to the heat and muscle behind his shirt, and somehow they couldn't stop sliding up to the big, broad shoulders that were on a higher level than hers, which was a new experience...reaching up to a man...and it sparked a swarm of previously thwarted female feelings...a man whose physique more than complemented her own too generous body length.

The temptation to feel what it was like with such a man as Nathan King—just this once—dissolved all the reasons why she shouldn't. It was only a kiss, which he was delicately deepening, inviting her active participation, promising a pleasurable exploration that would satisfy her curiosity. No force involved. No danger attached to it. She could back out any time she liked, dismissing the impulse to taste as inconsequential.

He knew how to kiss. He was very good at it. So distractingly good she was barely aware of his hands sliding around her waist, though her whole body was instantly and acutely conscious of his when he hauled her against him. But by then that was what she wanted, to feel more of him, revelling in the dominant maleness he emitted and incredibly excited by it.

Hungry, urgent kisses, a gathering passion for them, and her hands climbing, clutching his head, pulling him down to her, her body arching into his, pinned there by his hands, engulfed by a sweet storm of sensation, riding with it until the growing hardness of his wanting sparked some shred of sanity in her mind, and the shock of her susceptibility to Nathan King's attraction took hold.

She grabbed his ears and forced his head up. He stared at her, his eyes hot and glazed, steaming with rampant desire. She stared back, panic clutching her stomach where he was pressed so explicitly against her, panic screeching through her mind at having let this...this foolish experiment...go so far.

"You're right," he muttered gruffly. "Not the time or place."

Before she had wits to make any reply, he collected himself and moved, scooping her off her feet and lifting her onto the passenger seat of the helicopter as effortlessly as though she were some lightweight doll.

"Throw your hat and bag on the back seat," he instructed, and closed the door, sealing her into position.

Miranda was a trembling mess, her mind stuck in a maze of incredulity...unanswerable questions about herself and her totally inappropriate and shamingly intimate response to a man she barely knew and didn't want to know. Even now, her body was in revolt at having been deprived of what it had wanted from him.

Chemistry!

How did one switch it off?

One solution zipped through her squirming confusion. Get out of the helicopter! She didn't have to go with him or even be with him. She found the handle to open the door. Then a surge of pride insisted running away was not the most effective move to deal with this.

She had a choice to make here and she had to make Nathan King respect her choice. Her contract at King's Eden ran two years and there was no way of avoiding him for two years. A stand had to be taken. Words said. He had to be convinced there was never going to be a *right* time or place for what he wanted from her. No way was she going to fall into the Bobby Hewson trap again.

She'd barely remembered to toss her hat and bag onto the back seat before Nathan King hauled himself into the space beside her, triggering an awful sense of vulnerability. She fastened her seat-belt and did her utmost to ignore his impact on her senses as he settled himself.

"Have to get moving if we're to catch the sunrise," he said, handing her a set of headphones and linking up the electronics.

Thankfully he switched on the ignition and busied himself with getting them off the ground. Miranda donned the headphones, which drowned out the noise and allowed her to speak to him but decided any talking was best done later. After she had calmed down. When she could choose her words carefully, not in heat. And when being in the wretchedly small space of this helicopter didn't make her feel so *crowded* by him.

Determined on shutting him out for the duration of the flight, Miranda resolved to keep her gaze trained strictly on the view. Which was what she was here for...firsthand knowledge of tourist territory...and which she proceeded to do, once they were in the air.

All the same, even as she watched a seemingly endless vista of beige grass dotted by the grey-green foliage of the universally small outback trees, her nerves were strung taut, waiting for Nathan to say something. As time dragged by, she began to hate the thought he was simply sitting tight, congratulating himself on having sparked a positive response from her, and anticipating more of the same.

"You'll miss the approach if you keep looking out of the side window, Miranda."

The advice boomed into her ears, jolting her out of her dark brooding.

"That's the start of the Bungle Bungle Range straight ahead of us."

Relief poured through her at his matter-of-fact tone, and the moment she looked where he directed, his domination of her thoughts faded, her mind filling with the wonder of what lay before her.

She had seen photographs of Ayer's Rock, a huge monolith rising with stunning effect from a vista of flat land as far as the eye could see. The Bungle Bungle Range gave the same weird sense of not belonging to the general landscape, but it was much more than a monumental rock. It looked like some ancient remnant of a lost civilisation, embodying mysteries that no one knew the answers to any more.

The photographs in the pamphlet hadn't captured what she was seeing, couldn't capture the size and fascination of it. It seemed to rise out of nowhere, unconnected to anything else, a huge amalgamation of massive beehive structures, horizontally striped in orange and black. The rising sun vividly illuminated the orange sections and made the black more stark.

Miranda knew there were geological explanations for the colours—layers of silica and lichen—and the shapes. She'd read them in the pamphlet. Yet the stripes seemed so evenly spaced, as though to some deliberate, artistic plan, and the striations in the rock of some of the massive domes on the outskirts of the range gave her the impression of buildings built of bricks, like pyramids with the sharp edges having crumbled away over thousands and thousands of years.

She knew it was fanciful to ignore expert knowledge—this was all solid sandstone, and the formation was actually dated back three hundred and fifty million years—but she couldn't help envisaging ancient rulers being buried inside those time-worn domes.

"Had enough or do you want to see more?" Nathan asked evenly, not pushing either way.

"More, please," she answered, not grudging those words to him.

He flew the helicopter over the range in a criss-cross pattern, giving her every aspect of it. The narrow canyons or gorges had been carved by water, so she'd read, yet the rock-face it had carved was so smooth and sheer in places, the impression of narrow streets running deep down beside blocks of petrified, windowless skyscrapers kept flowing through Miranda's mind. If this was the work of nature, it had been wrought in incredible patterns.

"Time we landed if we're to keep our schedule," Nathan informed her.

"Okay," she conceded, realising he'd seen all this before and had been pandering to her interest, probably indulging her so she would be more ready to indulge him. And on the ground she would be more accessible to whatever he had in mind.

He set the helicopter down close to a group of buildings beyond the massif, presumably the park rangers' headquarters. Intensely wary of his intentions, Miranda swiftly unfastened her seat-belt, whipped off her headphones, opened the door on her side and was out before Nathan could *help* her, thereby avoiding any macho familiarity he might take, being bigger and stronger than she was.

"Forgot your hat and bag," he said, handing her the items as he joined her on the ground.

"Thanks," she mumbled, deeply vexed she hadn't thought of them in her hurry to get out. The omission revealed her distracted state of mind. "That was so fantastic from the air, I'm eager to see more of it from ground level," she rolled out as an excuse, not wanting him to think *he* was the cause of her haste.

"Worth catching the sunrise?" he remarked, his blue eyes glinting with amused mockery.

"Very much so."

"Sorry if I offended your dignity by bundling you into the helicopter back at the resort, but we were running short of time. Nature doesn't wait on anything. If we want it working for us we have to follow its dictates."

Which was a double-edged excuse if she'd ever heard one! If he thought she was going to take sexual dictation from nature, he could think again.

"I didn't ask for a delay to our departure, Nathan," she said pointedly.

"True!" He had the gall to grin. "But I didn't hear or feel any protest for quite some time. Which leaves us with a promising area to explore, doesn't it?"

"Only if the wish is there to explore it," she flashed back at him with a look that should have shrivelled his confidence.

It merely raised a quizzical eyebrow. "No problem on my side. Is there one on yours?"

She fixed some mockery of her own directly on him. "Just where do you see this exploration leading to?"

He made a playful frown. "Well, the start of it suggested we're onto something special together. And now you're throwing in some mystery. No doubt about a strong dash of excitement. Who can tell what will come out of it?''

He was laughing at her, making light of any possible reservations she might have about an open-ended future. Except it wasn't open-ended to her. She saw a very inevitable end.

''That sounds quite romantic. Except you know and I know there won't be any romance involved. I bet right now you're figuring on a two-year convenient affair. And I tell you right now—'' her voice hardened as she delivered the bottom line ''—I won't play.''

CHAPTER SIX

"PLAY?"

Nathan King's incredulous repetition of her word gave Miranda a queasy moment of doubt. Had she let her own fears paint a crass picture of what he intended?

She watched, with galloping trepidation, while his expression underwent several changes...disbelief shifting to reassessment, then distaste.

He couldn't have had anything serious in mind with her, she fiercely told herself. He just didn't like having his motives baldly laid out. Probably no other woman had ever knocked him back quite so bluntly or abruptly. New experience for him!

Just as his eyes took on a laser-like probe, a greeting rang out. They both turned to see a lean bearded man strolling towards them. The interruption was silently welcomed by Miranda. It broke the imminent threat of further confrontation with Nathan King and gave her the chance to regroup her defences.

The newcomer looked to be only in his early thirties and he viewed Miranda with speculative interest as Nathan introduced them. "Jim Hoskins, head park ranger, Miranda Wade, the new resort manager at King's Eden."

They shook hands but there was no opportunity for any conversation between them. Nathan claimed Jim's attention, withdrawing a parcel of books from his bag. "The diaries. Take good care of them, won't you?"

Jim took the parcel, handling it with reverential care. "I'm much obliged, Nathan. I'll treat them with the utmost respect. Hard to get any history on this area."

"Personal diaries aren't exact historical fact," Nathan drily warned. "My great-grandmother might have been fed tall tales by the Aborigines of the time. Generally white people weren't let into tribal secrets."

"Well, I'm sure I'll find them interesting anyway."

Miranda thought she would, too, but she could hardly ask for a loan of old family diaries from a man she was intent on rejecting.

"Come along," Jim invited, waving to the building. "I'll put tea or coffee on for you." He smiled at Miranda as she and Nathan fell into step with him. "Your first time here?"

"Yes. This is an amazing place."

"Unfortunately we're short of time, Jim," Nathan interjected.

Miranda tensed. Was that true, or was he impatient to get her to himself again?

"I promised to show Miranda Cathedral Gorge and have her back at the resort at noon," he explained. "I know she's eager to get on with the sight-seeing, so we'll pass up the coffee, if you don't mind. I've got some packed."

Which neatly cut the park ranger out of the agenda, using her own excuse for hurrying out of the helicopter. It was clear Nathan was not going to allow her to use Jim Hoskins as a buffer between them. Not even for a short time. Though to be fair, she didn't know how long it took to get to Cathedral Gorge.

Jim shrugged, accepting the argument without question. "Pity you're so rushed." He pointed to a heavy duty four-wheel-drive vehicle parked beside the road. "The Land Cruiser's ready to go. Keys in the ignition."

"Thanks, Jim. We'll be off then."

"No problem."

He parted company with them with a cheery wave and Miranda resigned herself to being alone with Nathan again.

They headed straight for the Land Cruiser, neither of them offering conversation. Miranda didn't look at Nathan but she was extremely conscious of purposeful energy radiating from him and knew he was going to contest her "no play" decision. But if he kept it to only words, she would cope, and she didn't have to be more than polite in her replies. Let him think whatever he liked. The only important thing was to maintain a safe distance.

He opened the passenger door for her. She stepped past him with a cool "Thank you," and heaved herself into the high cabin, noting that he didn't attempt to assist. Her independent exit from the helicopter had at least made that point.

He didn't speak even when they were on the road. In fact they travelled a considerable distance, the silence in the Land Cruiser growing more and more nerve-racking as the track they were taking got rougher and rougher, the four-wheel drive ploughing through deep sand, bumping over corrugations, traversing a rocky creek bed where running water could have made the crossing more perilous if he hadn't known which way to go.

There was no sign of anyone else now, no trace of any humanity in the ancient land around them. The clumps of spinifex and the high conical termite mounds added to the sense of life reduced to a minimal state. It was a far different world from the one she'd known all her life and she began to sense she was with a very different kind of man, too…a man who made his own rules.

She wasn't running this game.

He was.

At his own pace and on his own terms.

And that realisation sent a chill down Miranda's spine. His patient silence at the dinner table that first night, his patient silence in the helicopter, now in this Land Cruiser, waiting…waiting for what?

"You're right," Nathan said abruptly. "I'm not offering romance. I've been there, done that, and come out empty every time. Fool's gold."

The edge of contempt in his voice startled her into looking at him. He sliced her a hard, challenging glance, searing in its intensity. "Look around you," he directed, turning his gaze back to the hazardous track. "My life is bound up in this land. It comes down to basic needs and that is pervasive if you live here long enough. I have a great respect for basic needs. And sharing them makes sense to me."

Miranda frowned, realising he was talking of a stark reality he faced day after day. If basic needs weren't respected—and shared—survival could very well be at risk. She'd read stories of people who had perished in the outback, not appreciating all that could go wrong, nor comprehending the sheer isolation of great, empty distances—no ready help to call upon.

"Now I'd say there's something very basic between us that we could answer for each other," he went on.

One could survive without *sex*, Miranda silently argued, gritting her teeth against saying so, determined not to invite or encourage any conversation on that subject.

"A sharing. Not a taking," he emphasised.

Miranda remained stubbornly silent, her gaze trained out the side window, but she felt the hot, penetrating blast of his eyes on her and couldn't stop her muscles from tensing against it.

"I'm not interested in the games men and women play in the world you come from," he continued with a relentless beat that seemed to drum on her mind and heart. "I don't make promises I can't or won't keep. I'll say how it is for me. I want you, yes."

She didn't actually need that blunt honesty, having no doubts herself on that score.

"And you want me, Miranda."

That stung her into whipping her head around. "Oh, no, I don't!" she shot at him.

His eyes instantly and sharply derided her contention. "Deny it as much as you like, for whatever reasons you have, but it's not going to go away."

"Is that how you argued your last mistress into bed with you?"

"*Mistress?*"

His incredulity and the subsequent shake of his head

left Miranda furious with herself at having let those words slip. She snapped her gaze back to the road, willing him not to pick up on them, to simply let the whole matter drop.

No such luck!

"I don't know where you're coming from, Miranda," he said tersely, "but I am *not* married, and if I had a wife, I certainly wouldn't be seeking a mistress."

Mistress…lover…what was the difference when the arrangement was for sex on tap?

"The relationships I've had with women were all mutually desired and not one of them was an adulterous affair," he went on, his voice gathering an acid bite. "I happen to respect the commitment of marriage. A pity you don't."

"I beg your pardon!" Miranda hurled at him in bitter resentment of his judgement of her.

"So what happened?" he threw back at her. "The guy wouldn't leave his wife for you? Is that why you took the job at King's Eden, burning your boats?"

It was so close to the truth, a wave of humiliating heat scorched up Miranda's neck.

Nathan didn't miss it. He turned on more heat. "Or maybe you threw down the gauntlet and you're hoping he'll follow you up here. Which explains the no-go with me."

"This is none of your business!" she seethed.

"Well, I take exception to being coupled with a sleaze-bag who plays a game of deceit with the women in his life."

"Then please accept my apology." She managed to

get frost into her voice even though her face was still flaming.

"And it most certainly is Tommy's business if you're counting on breaking the two-year contract, should your lover toe your line."

"I have no intention of breaking it," she grated out. "And I do not appreciate all this supposition on your part."

"You opened the door, Miranda."

"And I'd take it kindly if you'd respect my choice to close it."

Blue eyes clashed with green in an electric exchange that sizzled the air between them. Miranda's heart thumped erratically. She could hear it in her ears, feel the strong throb of it in her temples. Goose-bumps rose on her skin.

"It's not a choice I can respect, but so be it," he said tersely, and broke the connection with her.

The ensuing silence was incredibly oppressive. Miranda felt totally drained of energy and miserable over the impression she'd left him with by not correcting his assumptions. Not that he had any right to make them!

Okay, she shouldn't have used the word, *mistress*, but it had been what Bobby had wanted of her, not what she had been. As for Nathan King, maybe she'd let her experience with Bobby Hewson colour her reading of his last relationship. On the other hand, he wasn't promising anything other than sex, which was all a mistress got from a man.

If there was one thing Miranda had learnt, it was she wanted to be valued for more than a roll in the hay. A roll with Nathan King might be…an interesting experience. Even special, she grudgingly conceded. But that wasn't enough for her. Especially not after Bobby Hewson. She wanted the kind of sharing that encompassed everything, the kind that led to marriage because no one else could fulfil that very special equation of wanting to be with each other. Exclusively! Which was hardly a likely prospect with Nathan King of the legendary King family.

Miranda was still brooding over this when the Land Cruiser came to a halt in open camping area on the outskirts of the Bungle Bungle Range. A four-wheel-drive wagon was parked close to four tents but they all seemed abandoned, no one in view anywhere.

"We hike in from here," Nathan stated. "The camping amenities block is kept clean. If you want to use it before we set out…"

"Yes, I will. Thank you."

She didn't wait for him to open her door. As she strode away from the Land Cruiser, she thought he probably hadn't intended to extend that courtesy to her anyway. A woman who didn't care about committing adultery didn't deserve his respect. Except she did care, and she hated having him think that of her.

No use telling herself it didn't matter, so long as it kept him away from her. It was a point of pride. And reputation. Though it went deeper than that, right down to her sense of self-worth.

She was not like her mother.

She was never going to be like her mother.

She needed to live her life on her own terms and somehow she had to make Nathan King understand that. And respect it.

CHAPTER SEVEN

MISTRESS!

Nathan brooded over his misconception of Miranda Wade as he waited for her to be ready for the trek into the gorge. Far from being a feminist, she was right at the other end of the scale, pleasuring married men. Of course, a woman with her looks would naturally attract wealthy targets whose egos were fed by having a mistress with such spectacular physical assets. And no doubt she'd profited by it. The dress she'd worn to dinner that first night undoubtedly had a designer label.

Was she turning the screws on some guy, putting herself out of easy reach by this shift to King's Eden? Or maybe she saw the resort homestead as a fertile hunting ground. The few select suites for guests there cost almost a thousand dollars a night. Anyone who could afford to stay for several days was in the millionaire class, and the managerial position put her in close proximity with them, hostessing dinner each night. It was a much more intimate footing than she'd get, managing a city hotel.

Nevertheless, despite whatever cool calculations went on in her mind, she had slipped up this morning. There *was* strong chemistry between them, however much she might want to dismiss it. Obviously he didn't have what she wanted out of life, so he was a waste of her time.

And, face it, man! She was a waste of his.

However frustrated he might feel about her ice beating the fire of this morning, pursuing the instincts still raging through him would only lead to more frustration. Best to let go right now. The last thing he needed was to be screwed up by a woman who was practised in deceit. Especially adulterous deceit.

The click of a door opening alerted him to her imminent return to his side. He half turned to watch her. She'd crammed her hat on her head so it came halfway down her forehead, shadowing her eyes. The rest of her still had the kick of a mule, but he was not going to be drawn by her lush femininity again. Let her sell it to the highest bidder. He was well out of that game.

He was looking at her as though she had crawled out from under some rock. Miranda instinctively stiffened her spine but her stomach was in a sickening knot. She cursed herself again for having allowed this man past her guard. Now here he was, standing in judgement on her, so formidable and forbidding she hated her vulnerability to what he thought of her. She shouldn't have to defend herself.

And she wouldn't.

She had apologised for misinterpreting his last relationship. Nothing more need be said on any personal score. She glanced at her watch as she neared where he stood waiting for her. It was almost eight o'clock. Only four more hours to get through with him.

"This way," he said, barely waiting for her to fall into step beside him before setting off.

Miranda kept her mouth firmly shut. The route into

the gorge was signposted. She didn't really need his guidance. In fact, she would have been better without it. He set such a brisk pace, she was so busy watching her footing over the rough ground, determined not to stumble or fall, there was little time for gazing around.

The beehive domes gradually amalgamated into a gorge whose walls rose higher and higher. As the walking track narrowed and the terrain became more difficult, Nathan took the lead with a muttered, "Best to follow where I tread."

As much as she bridled against his high-handed manner, there was nothing to be gained from disobeying. The sun had gathered heat and there was no shelter from it anywhere. Nathan unerringly chose the safest way over rocks and past tricky little chasms. A couple of times he paused to check if she needed a hand to negotiate an awkward ascent or descent but Miranda was proudly determined on not accepting any assistance.

Nevertheless, she reviewed her opinion about not needing a guide. The walk would have been much more hazardous and longer, picking her own way. As it was, she ended up misjudging her footing on a loose section of gravel at the top of a stony ridge, and as she took a steep step down to the next secure place, her back foot skidded out from under her, catapulting her straight towards the solid mass of Nathan King, who'd instantly swung at her yelp of distress.

She thumped into him, her hands automatically grabbing his arms to save her from falling in a heap at his feet. Not that she needed to worry about that. He reacted so fast, she found herself clamped to him, then hauled up his body until her feet found steady ground…between the legs he'd spread to anchor himself. But he didn't let her go…and she didn't let him go.

Her breasts were squashed against his chest and it felt as though their hearts were thundering in unison. Her pelvis and his seemed locked together, the key to his manhood fitting sensationally into the apex of her thighs. Her hands were wrapped around his biceps, loving their tensile strength. His vibrant heat and the sheer power of the man seemed to flood through her, holding her transfixed with a melting flow of insidious excitement.

She wasn't even aware that her hat had been knocked off. Her mind was abuzz with sexual signals that short-circuited all warning buttons. Her head tilted back, instinctively seeking more direct contact with him. The naked blast of desire in his eyes tore through the wanton glaze that had blinded her to what was happening. She sucked in a quick sobering breath through lips she realised were invitingly parted.

She saw his mouth compress, his jaw tighten and a savage mockery wiped the blaze of wanting from his eyes. He set her firmly apart from him, swept up her hat from where it had fallen and presented it to her.

"Better watch yourself more carefully, Miranda," he advised acidly. "Another slip like that…who knows what might get broken?"

Like her credibility in insisting she didn't want him.

"Thanks for saving me," she managed to mutter, cramming her hat back on to hide her burning face.

"Tommy needs you operational," he slung at her

before turning a broad, brick wall back and setting off again.

Miranda's legs felt like jelly. She forced them to work as they should, willing more energy into them. It wasn't fair, she thought, staring resentfully at the pumped-out strength of his stride. She'd gone weak from that treacherous embrace and he'd gained power. Nothing was fair where sex was concerned, she grimly concluded.

Twice now she'd succumbed to his attraction. He seemed to have some inbuilt magnet that got to her, overriding all common sense. She found herself eyeing the taut action of his buttocks and wrenched her gaze away. Somehow she had to switch off this *physical* thing with him, get her mind focused on her job again. Nathan King was not the object of this sight-seeing trip.

The rock edifice on either side of them was not striped as the domes were. The colours were still striking, a mixture of red and orange, yellow ochre, beige and black. Miranda was wondering why this was called Cathedral Gorge, when she heard the sound, a deep haunting throb that seemed to vibrate off the cliff walls in a weird unearthly rhythm. She stopped dead, absorbed with listening to it.

Nathan moved on a few steps, then turned, aware of her failure to follow. He frowned at her stillness, emitting impatience. He was about to voice it when she whipped up a hand to stop him.

"Don't you hear it?" she queried in an urgent whisper.

He nodded, his eyes glinting with ironic amusement at her enthralment.

It goaded her into asking, "What is it?"

"A didgeridoo being played against the cavern wall. Come on. You'll see it around the next bend. Albert must have decided to give the tourists a demonstration."

Albert?

A didgeridoo was an Aboriginal instrument. Did one of the tribes still live here?

Miranda sped after Nathan, eager to experience more of what she was hearing. And suddenly it came into view...the end of the gorge...a fantastic open cavern, the side walls towering up in incredibly sheer sheets of rock, the back one curved inward, sheltering a pool of mysterious black water surrounded by sand.

Behind the pool a group of six people sat on a jumble of flat rocks, watching an Aboriginal man blowing into a long hollow pole, the end of it resting on the ground as his hands moved over the holes in the wood, controlling the emissions of sound.

The eerie notes boomed up with all the power of a pipe organ in a cathedral, filling the cavern, echoing out like some primitive call that had passed through aeons of time, as though summoning the heartbeat of the earth itself so that those who heard it would feel its underlying rhythm and be in harmony with it.

It couldn't be called a song. There was no melody. Yet the interplay of sounds touched some deep soul chord that suddenly reminded Miranda of what Nathan had said earlier about his life being bound up in this land—ancient land—where survival reduced everything to basic needs.

She hadn't comprehended the full context of what he was saying but she had a glimmering of it now...the stark simplicity of choices laid out by nature, a cycle to be followed...birth, growth, mating, reproducing, death...an endless replenishment as long as the earth kept feeding it.

No romantic gloss.

Just life as it really was, underneath all the trimmings that civilisation had manufactured to sweeten it.

The playing ended on a long, deep, mournful note, which seemed to reverberate through Miranda, making her tingle in a shivery way. The Aboriginal man shouldered his didgeridoo. The group of six applauded, their enthusiastic clapping sounding totally wrong to Miranda, somehow trivialising an experience that should have been savoured in silence.

She was frowning over it when Nathan turned to look at her, his eyes hard and cynical. "The performance not worth your applause?"

She stared at him, feeling his contempt for the lack of understanding that connected what they'd just heard to a *performance* to be clapped. "Not everyone has your background, Nathan," she excused.

He raised an eyebrow. "You're not going to show some mark of appreciation?"

She struggled to express what she'd felt. "To me it was a communication, not a concert."

"Oh? And what did it communicate to you?"

His eyes were a pitiless blue, scorning any sensitivity from her. His challenge was a deliberate ploy to confirm the place he'd put her in—a woman without soul, a woman who cared only for herself, disregarding the hurt she might give to others.

Miranda's gaze bored straight back at him, resentment goading her into flouting his superficial and insulting reading of her character. "It gave me an insight into your life. And the life of those who have inhabited this land. How it must have always demanded they be attuned to its heartbeat."

Her reply visibly jolted him. His chin butted up as though hit by a punch of disbelief. His eyes flared as though she'd done serious violence to his feelings. For a few nerve-shaking moments, she felt caught in a fiercely questing force that tore at everything she was. Then just as suddenly it was withdrawn, Nathan turning away and walking on.

Denial? Frustration?

Feeling as though she'd been pulped and tossed aside, Miranda had to recollect herself *again* before following. The deep drifts of sand made walking heavy going, but clearly the cavern was their destination so there wasn't far to go now, and at least she wouldn't be *alone* with Nathan here.

Having consoled herself with this thought, she was dismayed to see the group of six getting to their feet and gathering up their bags. They trailed after the Aboriginal man who was skirting the pool and heading towards her and Nathan. Then she realised he was dressed in a tour guide uniform and had obviously been hired by these people to give them the benefit of his specialised knowledge.

"G'day, Nathan," he greeted familiarly, his face wreathed in a welcoming grin.

"G'day to you, Albert," came the warm reply, a tone of voice Miranda hadn't heard for some time. "You'll be haunting the tourists if you keep laying that on them."

The Aboriginal laughed as though it was a great joke. He patted his didgeridoo. "Only calling up good spirits." He flicked a twinkling glance at Miranda before adding, "Maybe you need them."

"Maybe I do," Nathan said with a nod of appreciation. "This is Miranda Wade. She's taken over management of Tommy's resort. Albert's a tribal elder around these parts, Miranda."

She offered her hand. "Thank you for playing. That was quite magical."

He shook it, his dark eyes shining happily at her comment. "Always good magic, Miss Wade. You staying on for a while?"

"Yes."

He released her hand and tipped his hat to Nathan. "Could be the right spirit for you, oldfella."

He strolled off, chuckling to himself. Nathan threw her a look that simmered with scepticism, then trudged on towards the pool. The sand firmed as they neared it, much to Miranda's relief. Albert's group passed them, breaking their conversation to say "Hi!" Miranda smiled and returned their greetings. Nathan merely nodded, though Miranda noted he drew long appraising looks from the women in the group.

Physically he'd have an impact on any woman, she thought, though he probably wouldn't expend his energy on many. An extremely self-contained man, she decided, watching him stride forward around the pool to the flat rocks which would undoubtedly serve as their resting place for refreshment. Everything about him seemed to shout *elemental male,* and it was true what he'd said, she couldn't deny his effect on her.

In a primitive society, he'd be the prize mate to get. No denying that, either. She had no doubt he could and would endure anything from this land, and still make it work for him. In some quintessential way, he belonged to it…as hard as these rocks, and just as unforgiving.

Maybe she was a fool to pass up an intimate involvement with him. Not that he was likely to give her a second chance after this morning's contretemps.

Might it have developed into something very special? Some wanton core in her pulsed yes and it was difficult to argue away. Nevertheless, she worked hard at it.

Sexual attraction was no assurance of anything working out well. And why should she believe what Nathan King said about himself and his relationships with other women? He'd undoubtedly bedded the woman who'd chosen to marry another man. What did that say about him?

He dropped his bag onto a large flat rock. Miranda settled for one about a metre short of his. Since the cavern shaded them from the sun, she took off her hat, welcoming the cooler air here. In an attempt to ignore the tension of having to share some inactive time with Nathan, she emptied her bag, placing the plastic container of melon, which she'd sliced into finger-size pieces on the rock between them, then taking a long drink from the bottle of mineral water everyone had told her to take, warning of dehydration.

"I have a thermos of coffee. Would you like some?" he asked.

"Yes. Please."

He used the same "table" rock to set out mugs and fill them, then produced two plastic containers of sandwiches. "Bacon, lettuce, tomato and cheese," he informed her. "You'll need something more substantial than melon. Help yourself."

"You, too," she invited.

They sat, munching and drinking in a loaded silence. Eventually Miranda decided to settle a harmless point of curiosity. "Why did Albert call you 'oldfella'? I wouldn't call you old."

"It relates to my family having been linked to this area for more years than Albert has lived. Longevity is counted in generations. Five generations here makes all of the Kings 'oldfellas.'"

"I see," she murmured, mentally kicking herself for even momentarily regretting her earlier rejection of him. A member of the King family would never seriously link himself with her, any more than a member of the Hewson family would, as Bobby had finally spelled out to her.

"What do you see, Miranda?"

She shrugged, meeting the searing question in his eyes with the inescapable fact she'd known from the beginning. "That I don't belong and you do."

"Where do you belong?" he asked.

She broke into laughter, shaking her head over the

emptiness of that question. "Nowhere. That's part of why I'm here. It doesn't matter where I am." She flashed him an ironic look. "I guess you could say I belong to myself."

He frowned and turned his gaze down to the pool below them. A dark, dark pool, Miranda thought, like her family background. Not that it could actually be called family, just her and her mother whose men had never offered a wedding ring...the whole sorry misery of it coming to a lonely end years ago. It was hardly the kind of history the King family would want attached to them in any shape or form.

"So you don't care about breaking up anyone else's sense of belonging."

The harsh remark was one too many for Miranda. "You have no right to probe into my personal life. I am here on a professional basis," she stated icily.

"You might have fooled my mother..."

She leapt to her feet, snapping with anger. "That's enough! I have never been a married man's mistress. Nor would I ever put myself in such a demeaning situation."

"Then what was all that mistress stuff about?" he shot back at her.

"It was about a man like you, wanting to put me in that position, and he had the power to mess up all I'd worked for. Just as you have the power to mess up my contracted time at King's Eden."

He was suddenly on his feet, a towering figure of proud indignation. "That's a hell of a thing to think of me!"

"Like the things you've being thinking about me,

huh? Treating me like dirt because I said *no play!*''
Her eyes raked his arrogant pride into meaningless tat-
ters. "Well, let me tell you I'm not about to take the
chance you're any different from him. I don't care how
sexy you are. I...won't...play!"

Her whole body was shaking with the vehemence of
that denial and her last three words boomed around the
cavern, echoing, echoing...out of her control. She'd let
him drive her out of control.

Desperate to grab some shreds of it back, she shoved
her drink bottle into her bag. Her hands fumbled over
the lid of the melon container. A hand clamped around
her wrist, stilling the agitated action.

"I promise you...I swear to you...your position at
King's Eden is safe from any interference from me."

Her heart was pounding so hard she couldn't bring
herself to speak at all. She stared down at the strong
brown fingers wrapped around her wrist, imprisoning
it.

"And please...accept my apology for making you
feel at risk. That was not my intention."

His voice seemed to throb with sincerity. She
couldn't look at him, couldn't tear her gaze from the
hold he had on her, his flesh imprinting itself on hers,
fingers pressing on her pulse, his energy zipping into
her bloodstream, imparting an indelible sense of joining that wasn't true. It couldn't be true.

"As for what I thought of you...I'm glad I was
wrong. And I apologise for that, too. Believe me
now...you are safe with me, Miranda. Okay?"

She nodded, too choked by a tumult of emotion to
do anything else. He released her and began repacking

his bag. Miranda concentrated hard on finishing with hers.

Her mind thrummed with the knowledge that she didn't feel *safe* with Nathan King and never would. He was more than Bobby Hewson. Much more. And even if he left her alone, as he promised, she would not stop being acutely aware of him and the power he had to reach into her.

Neither of them said anything throughout the hours it took to journey back to the resort. There was no touching, physical or verbal. Miranda did her utmost to block him out of her personal space but he kept infiltrating it just by the sheer force of his presence.

For all her practised professionalism, she found herself hopelessly tongue-tied when she finally had to face him on the helipad at King's Eden. She forced her gaze to meet his and almost flinched at the intense blue of his eyes as they probed hers.

"Thank you," she blurted out, barely stopping herself from backing away from him.

"Miranda, I have nothing to do with the resort and Tommy would certainly not welcome any interference from me in his business," he stated emphatically. "It's entirely up to you to make good your position here."

She nodded, her throat too constricted to speak.

"You want time to feel settled into your job…fine!" he went on. "But I don't see myself forgetting what there is between us. And I don't think you will, either."

She did not answer, feeling the threat to her peace of mind and not knowing what to do about it.

"I'll see you again sometime," he added, and took his leave of her.

She watched him get into his Jeep and drive away.
Only when he was out of sight did she begin to breathe
easily. Two years at King's Eden, she thought. Of
course she would see him again...sometime. And what
then?

What then?

CHAPTER EIGHT

IT WAS good to see Jared again. Nathan reflected that he always had enjoyed his youngest brother's company. Tommy had a competitive streak, wanting to score points on everything, while Jared was simply content to be himself, not in contest with either brother. Maybe it was because he'd moved himself into their mother's world, away from King's Eden. Or maybe it was simply his nature.

They sat in the breakfast room, idling over morning tea, Jared and their mother relaxing after their flight from Broome, Nathan catching up on their recent activities. Tommy would fly in this afternoon and would inevitably draw Jared's attention to himself, but for the moment, it was very pleasant listening to his youngest brother's plans to extend the pearl business from wholesale into retail, as well.

"So how goes it with you, Nathan?" he asked, the conversation having lulled after he and their mother had filled him in on their news.

"Oh, nothing really changes here," he drawled, except he only had half his mind concentrated on station business. Miranda Wade occupied the other half, but he wasn't about to lay out that very private issue.

In fact, he was thinking this family get-together on the station—the first this year—may very well provide the opportunity to get him close to Miranda again, in

73

a non-threatening social situation, which would surely ease her fears.

"Mum tells me we have a new manager at the resort," Jared prompted. "A woman."

"Yes." A woman who haunted his nights and wouldn't get out of his head even during the day.

"So how is she working out?"

"I have no idea." Which was really a lie. He'd envisaged her a thousand times, burning with utter commitment to getting everything right at the resort, shutting out everything else from her mind. Including him. Especially him. Though he didn't believe she could be any more successful than he was at setting aside the strong attraction they'd experienced. All the same, the need to know wouldn't wait much longer.

"Don't you have some impression, Nathan?" his mother asked, frowning at him.

"Why should I? I don't stick my nose into Tommy's business any more than I stick it into Jared's."

His mother's gaze sharpened on him. "You did take Miranda on a sight-seeing trip, didn't you?"

"Six weeks ago," he answered with a shrug. "I haven't seen her since."

His mother sighed, looking extremely vexed.

"I'm sure Tommy will fill you in when he arrives this afternoon." Nathan smiled at her, seeing a way to use her frustration. "You can grill him to your heart's content," he added casually.

It earned an exasperated glare. "I wanted another point of view."

"Then why not ask Miranda over to dinner tonight, satisfy yourself about her? Satisfy Jared's curiosity, too. You could ask Sam, as well. Get her opinion. Make a party of it.''

''Yes,'' his mother snapped, looking at him as though she wanted to box his ears. ''I shall do that, Nathan. I'll get some answers for myself since I can't count on either you or Tommy to be sensible about women.''

Her eyes glittered bitter disapproval.

He thought fleetingly of Susan, aware his mother had considered her a waste of his time. But mothers didn't know everything. All the same, he was glad that door was shut now because another door had opened and it had a stronger lure than any he had ever known.

''Well, it's lucky you can count on Jared to be sensible,'' he tossed out, then slanted a teasing grin at his brother. ''Been a good boy, have you?''

He laughed and they moved onto a lighter vein of conversation, which suited Nathan just fine since he only had to give half his mind to it.

Tonight, he thought with deep satisfaction.

Tonight he would find out more about the woman he wanted.

As was her custom, Miranda was ready to welcome back the homestead guests as they returned from their day's activities. She waited on the verandah, watching the fishing party unload themselves from the Jeep Sam always commandeered, and thinking they looked well satisfied with what they had chosen to do.

''Look at these great barramundi!'' John Trumbell crowed, holding up his catch for her to admire as he led the others up the path.

Miranda laughed at his glee. "Biggest I've seen this season, John."

Robyn, his wife, asked. "Can we give them to the chef to cook for our dinner tonight?"

"Of course. Should make a great feast for you."

"It was a marvellous day," Robyn enthused. "I've never gone fishing in a helicopter before." She swung around to Sam who was trailing after them. "Thanks for the ride."

"Couldn't get you to that part of the river any other way," Sam informed her.

Robyn sighed happily, turning to the other couple who had accompanied her and her husband. "Don't you just love the outback? It was like fishing in a world of our own."

The others made equally enthusiastic comments as they passed Miranda. Sam sidled up to her and remarked sotto voce, "Wonderful, when you've got money to burn."

She grinned. It was true the guests who took homestead suites never seemed to count the cost of anything. Nevertheless, in the month since the resort opened, she'd found that even the campers loved being here, just exploring the gorges, swimming in waterholes, enjoying the unique wildlife.

"So what's on for tomorrow?" Sam asked, rolling her eyes.

"For them the Bungle Bungle Range."

"Got Albert lined up to take them in after I've landed them?"

"Of course."

Miranda's mind flinched away from the memory of

her morning with Nathan. It still haunted her, even after six weeks of seeing nothing of him. It seemed he had decided to respect her choice not to play. The problem was, in the lonely hours of the night, she was tormented by the question of what might have been if she'd chosen differently.

"Someone coming," Sam remarked, squinting past Miranda at a Jeep, which was fast approaching. "Looks like Tommy. Must be coming from the station homestead. Are you expecting him?"

"No, I'm not." She was puzzled by this unheralded visit. "He dropped in on Tuesday to check through everything with me."

Sam gave her a crooked smile. "Well, it's Saturday. Maybe he's without a date tonight and hopes you'll fill in."

"Then he'll be out of luck."

Sam shook her head in bemusement. "It's an education, watching you block him out. Mind if I stay to watch the fun?"

"As you like."

She didn't find Tommy's flirtatiousness fun, and didn't really see what fun Sam could get out of watching them together. Apparently it amused her, yet Miranda kept remembering what Nathan had said about Sam's feelings for Tommy, and she couldn't help thinking it was masochistic to want to watch. Or maybe it was a case of not being able to help herself. If he was like a magnet to her...

A convulsive little shiver ran down Miranda's spine. It had certainly been easier, throwing herself into her job and getting on top of it with Nathan out of sight, if not completely out of mind. Tommy was not a problem to her. His irrepressible personality seemed to bounce around her personal sidesteps and he never pushed beyond the boundaries she set. Getting the business right came first with him and he wasn't about to upset that applecart.

"How's it going?" he called cheerily as he came up the path.

"Fine!" Miranda answered.

He stopped short of the verandah, looking up at them with a quizzical little smile. "Mum and Jared have flown in for the weekend. You are commanded to come to dinner at the station homestead tonight."

She frowned. "Commanded?"

Her heart started skittering. Nathan had *commanded?*

"Invited," Tommy corrected wryly. "But take it from me, there's no ducking out of my mother's invitations."

His mother, not Nathan.

Her mind started skittering.

Did Tommy think she ducked out of *his* invitations? Why couldn't he simply accept her disinterest? Was he behind this *command?* Was Nathan? Was it simply Elizabeth King dictating her own desire to check the situation at the resort?

Why couldn't they simply let her be? She was doing a good job. Yet she felt an irresistible tug at the thought of meeting Nathan again…what it might mean…

It would be safe, she reasoned. Had to be safe with Elizabeth King there, and the other brother, Jared. It might even dispose of the wanton thoughts that plagued her lonely nights…show her beyond question how foolish any involvement with him would be.

"What about our guests here?" she prevaricated, feeling hopelessly at odds with a desire she *knew* could lead nowhere good.

"Spend Happy Hour with them," Tommy promptly replied. "Settle them at the table, and leave them to their own devices. They know each other from last night, don't they?"

He'd checked the bookings earlier in the week and all four couples in the homestead suites overlapped this weekend. "I won't be able to leave here until after seven," she pointed out.

"That's understood. We'll be dining at eight." He slid Sam a teasing look. "Mum said for you to come, too, squirt. Balance the table."

"Oh, sure! I can just hear Elizabeth saying that," she scorned.

"Well, I told her you probably didn't have a dress to wear."

"I'll put one on especially for Jared." She cocked her head on one side. "Or maybe I'll make a play for Nathan, now that Susan's out of the picture."

Susan…Miranda found her hands clenching and consciously relaxed them. Susan might not have been Nathan's *mistress,* but he hadn't married her. *Don't forget that!*

Tommy laughed and bounded up the steps, ruffling Sam's copper curls as he passed. "Go get him, Red!" Then to Miranda, "I'll just have a word with Roberto. He can come out of his kitchen between courses and wax lyrical about what he's cooked for the guests. Keep them happy.''

They watched him head off inside, mission accomplished as far as they were concerned.

"One of these days I'm going to kick him in the shins," Sam muttered.

It drew an instant wave of sympathy. Both of them fools over men. "You have beautiful hair," Miranda quietly assured her. "If you ask me, Tommy couldn't resist touching it.''

She heaved a rueful sigh. "I bet no man has ever ruffled your hair, Miranda.''

"I haven't had the easy-going kind of friendships you've made. I rather envy you that.''

It drew a speculative look that Miranda instantly shied away from, not wanting to answer questions about her life. She glanced at her watch. "Better get moving. Are you going to accompany me to the commanded dinner or go over earlier by yourself?''

"I'll wait for you. I'll get one of the resort Jeeps and have it out here at seven-fifteen. Okay?''

"Yes. Thanks, Sam.''

"You'll like Jared," she remarked, still with that speculative look.

"We'll see," Miranda returned non-committally.

It wasn't Jared on her mind as she headed off to get ready for tonight. It wasn't Jared or Tommy or Elizabeth King playing havoc with her pulse rate and tying knots in her stomach.

Nathan...his name was like a drumbeat on her heart.

Tonight she would see him again.

And she wanted it to be right.

But how could it be?

It was mad to think it...mad to want it...yet despite every bit of hard, common sense reasoning...there was no denying what she felt.

CHAPTER NINE

IT WAS Tommy, not Nathan, who greeted them at the door and ushered them inside. As they moved towards the lounge room, the usual snippy repartee went on between him and Sam but it floated over Miranda's head. Every nerve in her body was screwed tight, waiting with an excruciating awareness of her own helpless fever-pitch anticipation, to feel whatever she would feel when she came face-to-face with Nathan King again.

Then they entered the room where he had to be...and he wasn't there. The big black leather armchair where he'd been sitting that first night was unoccupied. Elizabeth King was sitting in *her* chair. A tall young man—the third brother?—had risen from the nearby chesterfield and was holding his arms out in welcome. No one else was in the room!

Sam rushed forward and into Jared's offered embrace with all the gusto of an excited puppy, delighted to see a much-missed loved one. While she was being whirled around, admired and kissed, a strange, blank feeling descended on Miranda, stilling all the wild agitation this visit had set in motion.

She wasn't aware of having come to a dead halt, wasn't aware of Tommy lingering at her side, wasn't aware of Elizabeth King watching her. For several empty moments, she didn't know what she was doing

82

here. The whole focus of her coming was lost. Nathan wasn't even present.

Then Tommy nudged her elbow, and her mind clicked into a different alert phase. It was Elizabeth King who had commanded her presence and there was another brother to meet. It took a giant effort to recollect herself, to smile at Nathan's mother, to move forward for the introduction Tommy obviously wanted to make. The older woman, dressed in a pale green shift tonight, and the pearls she seemingly always wore, dipped her head in a gracious acknowledgement.

Miranda had chosen to wear white, wanting Sam to feel she outshone her, which Sam did in a bright blue clingy dress that enhanced the colour of her eyes. Whether Sam's glamorised appearance had the desired effect on Tommy, Miranda neither knew nor cared at the moment. His voice seemed to boom in her ears, accentuating the hollowness inside her.

"Jared, if you wouldn't mind freeing yourself from the sex-kitten clinging onto you..."

The man with Sam grinned at him. "Jealous, Tommy?"

"Wait for the claws, little brother. That kitten can deliver lethal scratches."

"Oh, there are some guys who can make me purr," Sam tossed at him, purring so exaggeratedly it made both men laugh.

Miranda managed to keep a smile pasted on her face and tried to inject interest into her eyes as Tommy proceeded to present her to his brother.

"This is my resort manager, Miranda Wade. And Sam's victim for the night is my brother, Jared, the jet setter, who has deigned to touch down with us this weekend.''

"Now, Tommy, you know you wear the title of King of the Air. I'm merely a passenger," Jared remarked good-humouredly as he offered his hand to Miranda, smiling into her eyes. "I'm delighted to meet you."

"Thank you. It's a pleasure to meet you, too, Jared."

She forced her mind to gather impressions. Of the three sons, he most favoured his mother in looks, the same deep brown eyes, high cheekbones, straight aristocratic nose. His thick black hair dipped over his forehead in an attractive wave, softening what was a rather lean face. He was slightly taller than Tommy, not as tall as Nathan, and his slim physique seemed to carry a whip-chord strength rather than solidly built muscle.

"I hope it will be," he said, projecting warm friendliness. "Some people find our family a bit daunting en masse. Sam is used to us—" he withdrew his hand and put his arm around her shoulders, giving her a smile and a hug "—virtually grew up with us..."

En masse? The phrase jolted Miranda. Would Nathan be joining them?

Unaccountably her skin began prickling. Her attention drifted from what Jared was saying. As though tugged by some invisible force, her head turned...and he was there, bringing with him a current of energy that blasted everyone else out of Miranda's consciousness.

Her body instantly reacted to how big he was, how male he was, and a shock wave of memory supplied how he'd felt pressed close to her...the power and the strength of the man tapping on instincts that responded in full flood. An aching weakness spread through her, threatening every bit of composure she'd managed to harness.

She watched his approach with a sense of helpless vulnerability, belatedly realising he was carrying a tray of drinks from an adjoining room and not really targeting her.

"Champagne cocktails for everyone," he announced, drawing enthusiastic replies from the rest of the party.

Miranda stood dumbly, feeling his deep voice thrum into her bloodstream, kicking her heart into a wild gallop. He made good-humoured comments to everyone as he offered the tray, first to his mother, then to her and Sam. Miranda took a glass before caution could whisper she shouldn't consume anything so potent as a champagne cocktail. The men took their drinks and Nathan made a toast.

"To a happy evening together."

Tommy and Jared kept topping that toast in a stream of witty repartee. Sam and Elizabeth King laughed at them. Nathan casually moved aside, placing himself directly in front of Miranda.

"Would you prefer iced water?" he asked. "I've just remembered..."

"No, this is fine, thank you," she rushed out so fast her voice sounded breathless. Her gaze was stuck at the gleaming V of brown flesh revealed by his open-necked shirt. She had to force it up, feeling dreadfully unprotected as the force of his dangerously discerning gaze hit hers. "Drinking a toast with iced water isn't quite the same, is it?'' she said in a more moderate tone.

He smiled. ''The choice is yours.''

Her mind seized on his seemingly deliberate use of the word, *choice*. His smile was inviting, encouraging, or was she so giddy from trying to control her own desires she was misreading his intention?

''This will do for now,'' she said, sipping the cocktail gingerly.

''Good! Is the resort working out as you wanted?''

''Everything is running very smoothly at the moment.''

His smile took on an ironic curl. ''My mother was extremely vexed I knew nothing to tell her. Tommy, incidentally, gave a glowing report.''

''I'm glad he's pleased with my management.''

''No question about that,'' he assured her, though his eyes seemed to burn with questions.

Miranda could feel herself flushing. Did he think she had Tommy dangling on a string? ''I like my work,'' she said defensively.

''My mother will be glad to hear it. She likes to check things for herself.''

Was he excusing himself from having anything to do with this command invitation? Letting her know she was still *safe* from him? Subtly directing her to where she should be *right now!*

Her gaze shot to Elizabeth King and her cheeks grew hotter at the realisation that the older woman was keenly observing her. Distracted by Nathan, Miranda had ignored her hostess, and was probably being judged wanting in good manners. It was all the more embarrassing, with Nathan actually hinting where her place was.

"Please excuse me," she gabbled, and made a bee-line for Elizabeth King, concentrating fiercely on how to minimise her gaffe.

She was graciously welcomed to the seat beside Elizabeth and remained there, doing her utmost to redeem herself in the older woman's eyes until dinner was called. Not that she was subjected to a cross-examination of business angles. The conversation seemed more directed towards her feelings about King's Eden, apparently determining how settled or unsettled she was in her new location. Miranda hoped her replies gave satisfaction. It was impossible to stop the dreadful churning in her stomach.

When they moved into the dining room, she was expecting to be placed next to Elizabeth. It was disconcerting—the purpose of her being here thrown out of kilter again—when she and Sam were directed to flank Nathan at the end of the table with Tommy and Jared on either side of their mother.

A balanced table... Tommy's comment flitted through Miranda's mind, yet it didn't feel right to her. The three King brothers and Sam shared a long familiarity. She was the outsider, placed in their midst but not a part of them, and that feeling deepened as dinner progressed and the others talked of people and events she had no knowledge of.

This was a world that was closed to her, she kept thinking, and she would never belong to it. Somehow she would have to stifle the feelings Nathan stirred in her. As it was, being seated so close to him was a nagging torment. Every movement he made, every word he said, burned more brightly on her consciousness than anything else.

When Jared started asking questions about her experience in the hospitality business in the city, compared to the situation she was handling now, she responded eagerly to his interest, welcoming a conversation that took her mind off Nathan. Tommy moved the topic onto tourism, and Sam brought up comments from her parents who were currently touring Argentina.

"What about your family, Miranda?" Nathan suddenly inserted, making her heart leap and her head jerk towards him.

He offered a sympathetic smile. "You're in the midst of ours. Sam's been rattling on about hers. I guess it's made you feel a bit homesick for yours."

"Not at all," she denied, confusion whirling through her mind again. Why was he asking? She'd told him she didn't belong anywhere. Despite the smile, his eyes seemed to be gleaming with purpose.

"Well, no doubt they'll be coming to visit you," Jared suggested.

Shaken by Nathan's unexpected and forceful focus on her, Miranda was slow to respond to his brother.

Sam leapt in. "Have you got any scrumptious bachelor brothers that might drop in?" she asked, picking up the ball she'd been playing against Tommy all night.

"No," Miranda answered with what she hoped was discouraging brevity.

"Sensational sisters?" Tommy countered.

"I have no family," she stated bluntly, cornered into revealing that much.

Sam goggled at her. "You were an orphan?"

How could she stop this rolling inquisition? "I wasn't as a child. I simply have no family now," she said with emphatic finality.

"You mean they were all wiped out in some terrible accident?"

"Sam," Nathan cut in tersely, his frown chastising her for avid curiosity, which might lead into painful areas.

"Sorry!" She grimaced an apology. "Guess I've drunk too much champagne." Her eyes appealed to Miranda. "It's just you've been such a mystery, never mentioning anything personal in your past."

The comment focused even more interest on her and Miranda realised it would linger if it went unanswered, casting an awkward mood for the rest of the evening. Besides, what did it really matter? What point was there in hiding the fact she had no family pedigree whatsoever, nothing at all to recommend her to this company, apart from the business connection?

"There's no great mystery, Sam," she said with a casual shrug. "Unlike you and everyone else here, I have no family history going back generations. My mother was an orphan. I was her only child. She wasn't married and never did marry. I wasn't told who my father was and my mother died some years ago. So you see, I have very little to talk about."

An appalled silence followed this little speech. Miranda found it so unnerving, she felt a compelling urge to fill it in with more talk, minimising the great black hole in her life they were probably all envisaging.

"Family is not a factor in my life, but it's been very enlightening listening to all your news and the long connections between the Connellys and the Kings. It's very different from what I've known myself."

She tore her gaze from the miserable embarrassment on Sam's face and steeled herself to look straight at Nathan who'd started this spotlight on her, digging under her skin again. She might as well hammer home the point that she was an unsuitable match for a King, and knew it too well to imagine any personal relationship between them could be viable.

"The framed photographs along your hallway here...such a history must be fascinating to have...to look back on...to feel a part of..."

"Yes," he agreed, his eyes burning back a relentless challenge. "And most remarkable are the women who chose to follow their men here and make a life with them on this land. Like Sarah, who ran a brothel in Kalgoorlie, before throwing her lot in with Gerard."

"Sarah? Who wrote the diaries?" Miranda couldn't believe it.

"Yes. You might find them interesting to read sometime."

It must be true, Miranda thought dazedly.

"Then there was Dorothy, a governess on one of the cattle stations in The Territory," he went on. "One of nine children whose family was so poor she was virtually sold into slave labour. One less mouth to feed."

He paused to let that information sink in, his eyes mocking any sense of grandeur about his family.

"Irene was the wife of a stockman who was thrown from his horse and died of a broken neck. She had nowhere to go. No one to turn to. She stayed here and married Henry King."

"But that was in the old pioneering days," Miranda finally found wits enough to protest. "I daresay there weren't so many women then who would want to cope with such a life."

"Not so many women now, either," Nathan snapped back at her.

"I'm sure you're wrong. The status is very different now." She swung her gaze pointedly to Elizabeth King whose necklace of pearls was probably worth a fortune. "Wouldn't you agree?"

"It's true there are many long-established families in the Kimberly, which give them a kind of status rating over relative newcomers," she said consideringly. "But our population is so small...what is it, Nathan? Thirty thousand people in an area that covers over three hundred thousand square kilometres?"

"And that clustered mostly around the six major towns," he said in affirmation.

"For the most part, the outback rule still holds," Elizabeth King went on. "It's not so much who you are or where you come from, but what you accomplish *here* that earns respect and status."

For the most part..., Miranda silently noted that reservation.

"In fact," Tommy chimed in, "there are so many people with checkered pasts in the Kimberly, it's wiser to accept them at face value than to inquire too closely."

"The last outpost of civilisation," Jared said with a grin.

"Full of colourful characters," Tommy tagged on.

"But it does take time to earn respect and status," Miranda said, cutting to the heart of the matter. "The King family has an investment of a hundred years here. And I understand the pearl farms in Broome have been held by the same families for a similar length of time."

"And have been through as many ups and downs as those working the land," Elizabeth replied with a wry smile. "When I married Lachlan, all pearling activity in Broome had been virtually dead for years. Mother-of-pearl shell had been the main source of income and that had been undercut by the introduction of the plastic button. It wasn't until the advent of the cultured pearl that the farms built into the multimillion dollar business they are today. In marrying me, Lachlan got...only me."

Her gaze moved to Nathan, the dark brown eyes boring straight at her eldest son. "My life was with your father. He was where I wanted to be. It wasn't until after he died that I returned to Broome and involved myself in the pearl farming. You were old enough to take over from him, Nathan. You know you were. And that was what I couldn't bear...not King's Eden... King's Eden without Lachlan."

She paused, as though waiting for some critical comment from him. The sense of some running issue between mother and son was very strong. Miranda's mind spun with possibilities. Had Nathan judged his mother harshly for leaving? Had her departure triggered a mistrust in any woman being content to stay here, since not even his mother would? Was that why he had affairs rather than attempt a serious relationship?

She risked a covert glance at him. His face was like granite, revealing nothing. His eyes were narrowed, their expression veiled by lowered lashes, but his gaze was fixed on his mother. The silence was filling up with tension when he finally spoke.

"You did what you wanted to do," he said quietly. "I have no quarrel with that." He paused a moment, then added, "Trying to make people do what they don't want...is a fool's game...don't you think? It never gets the result we'd like."

Miranda felt the words, as though they were directed at her, reinforcing his claim that he would never manipulate a pressure situation to get what he wanted from her. She darted a glance at him but his gaze remained trained on his mother...a silent clash of wills that probably had nothing to do with her at all.

"Choices are always influenced by other things," came Elizabeth's pointed reply. "Which is why the *other things* need re-examining at times."

"On that I am in total agreement with you."

His gaze slid to Miranda, and the knowledge thumped into her heart that he was aware of the effect of his words on her, and every one of them was designed to reshape her view of him.

"I get the impression you're applying to us the kind of value system that operates in a more sophisticated society than we have here," he said with an ironic little smile. "Is that so, Miranda?"

Was he implying that wealth and power didn't count in their lives, in the associations they made?

"You can hardly say your name doesn't carry weight in the Kimberly," she asserted, unconvinced that such status was meaningless to this family, despite the examples they had cited.

His eyes mocked her reading of their situation. "It carries the weight of survival...which is what is most valued here."

"That's true," his mother cut in, swinging attention back to her. "The Kings, the Connellys, and my own family are survivors. It takes a certain breed of people—those I'd call of gritty character—to hold on in the Kimberly...to ride the good with the bad. There's no red carpet, Miranda. If I'd thought you were a red carpet person at heart, I would not have hired you for King's Eden."

"I see," she murmured, relief seeping through her at the realisation she wasn't viewed as an outsider by Elizabeth King, but as someone with the capability of being an insider. "I shall take that as a compliment."

"I might add that none of what we have now will survive unless there's a next generation." Her dark eyes glittered at Nathan and then moved to Tommy. "What will all your work and enterprise be worth then?"

"We're not exactly old men," Tommy protested jokingly.

"Time doesn't wait," his mother warned. "People always think there's plenty of time. Take it from me, Tommy, time runs out and what has been postponed never happens."

"Ah, now we're getting back to choice," Nathan

drawled. "Do we seize the day or plan for the future? What do you think, Miranda?"

He was zeroing in on her now, pouring out a current of energy that wound around her and tugged on the desire to pursue whatever might develop between them. Her pulse rate accelerated so quickly she felt dizzy. It was decision time. She could turn him off with her reply or open the door. Denial or risk?

His mother's words drummed through her mind... *time running out...opportunities lost...* She didn't know what her life was moving towards, didn't know if Nathan King could become an important part of it. All she knew was she no longer wanted to deny the chance that he might.

"I think I would like to read Sarah's diaries," she said, playing the safest line she could while inviting more contact with him.

For a moment it seemed she'd startled him. Then his eyes started dancing in amusement and his mouth widened into a grin. "I think you'll find your interest rewarded. I'll bring them over to you as soon as Jim Hoskins returns them."

"Thank you. I'd appreciate it."

He laughed, a ripple of joyous warmth that was far more intoxicating than a champagne cocktail.

Whether it was triggered by pleasure or triumph or simply amusement at the way she had answered him, Miranda couldn't tell. He was stunningly handsome when he laughed, his face alive with magnetic vitality, and it shot a wild zing of elation through her.

He *was* special.

She couldn't be feeling like this if he wasn't.

And right at this moment, she didn't care what the cost might be of knowing more of him.

CHAPTER TEN

DAY after day Miranda reminded herself she could not expect to see Nathan until Jim Hoskins returned Sarah's diaries, yet no amount of reasoning lessened the anticipation zinging through her mind, the excitement that fluttered through her every time she thought of being with him, and each day she felt a twinge of disappointment that he hadn't come.

When she lay in bed at night, she mentally replayed every minute of the dinner party at the station homestead, interpreting and re-interpreting Nathan's every word and action.

There was no doubt in her mind he had meant to push for another chance to move into her life, and when she'd given it, he was wise enough, or clever enough, not to capitalise on it too much, too soon. In fact, after he'd won what he wanted, he'd turned the dinner conversation back to general topics until they all rose from the table to have coffee and liqueurs back in the lounge room.

Then had come his casual offer to give her a personal tour of the photographs in the hallway. He'd pointed out the people he'd spoken of, giving a quick potted history of their lives on the cattle station, told a few amusing stories about them, and answered Miranda's questions without once attempting to seize any advantage with her.

97

There was no physical touching. Nevertheless, every time their eyes met, it felt as though he was reaching into her, stamping himself more and more irrevocably on *her* life and drawing her into his. The power of it was both exhilarating and frightening. Even when she and Sam left, she could feel it following her...desire that somehow tunnelled deeper than any desire she'd known before.

To Miranda's secret relief, Sam hadn't noticed anything *special* occurring with Nathan, or she was reserving comment on it. Neither Tommy nor Jared had shown any awareness that a shift had taken place between their brother and the new resort manager. Even Elizabeth King had seemed content with the evening at the end of it.

Of course, this *privacy* wouldn't last...couldn't once Nathan made his next move. This was a small community. People were going to notice and talk. But at least Nathan wasn't directly involved with the resort business, and the way he'd kept away from her so far proved there would be no unpleasantness at work, should a relationship between them not go well. Though she couldn't help hoping it would be something special. Really special.

As it happened, no amount of thinking prepared her for the circumstances that hit her on Thursday afternoon, just five days after she'd opened an invitational door to Nathan King. She'd done the rounds of the resort, checking that all accommodations levels were up to standard for the heavily booked weekend ahead, and supplies were more than adequate to meet demand. It was just past four o'clock when she entered her administration office, and without warning, the new world she'd begun to believe was free from her past, was suddenly attacked by it.

Val Warren, her clerical assistant, greeted her with a happy grin. "That cancellation we had on one of the homestead suites for this weekend…it's been taken up. We've got a full house again."

"Great! Short notice, though."

"I guess people who stay here can afford to be spontaneous," Val reasoned.

"Lucky for us! I'll have to check with Roberto that he's got enough gourmet food for the extra guests. What are their names?"

Val looked back at her monitor screen. "Married couple, currently staying at the Ayer's Rock resort, chartering a plane to fly directly here tomorrow, expected arrival time three o'clock…and their names are Celine and Bobby Hewson."

Miranda could feel the blood draining from her face. "Right!" she said weakly, and spun out of the office before Val saw the shock she'd delivered.

For several moments she leaned back against the closed door, fighting to recover some equilibrium. Maybe it was another Bobby Hewson whose wife just happened to be named Celine. They weren't uncommon names. Ayer's Rock, where they were currently staying, was like an Australian Mecca for tourists…the ancient red heart of the continent…but she couldn't imagine the Bobby she knew wanting to go there. But what about his wife? If she had accompanied him to Sydney…a honeymoon sight-seeing trip…

Wife… Miranda shook her head. Surely they weren't

even married yet. The engagement had only been announced three months ago. Shouldn't it take longer than that to arrange a big society wedding? It had to be some other couple. Had to be…

There was one way of settling any uncertainty. Galvanised into action, Miranda strode down the hall to her live-in quarters, intent on putting through a private call to the manager of the Ayer's Rock resort. The Bobby Hewson she knew would not be an unobtrusive guest. He would demand the best suite, the best service, and would let the manager know precisely who he was and what he stood for.

Once inside her self-contained apartment, Miranda moved straight to the telephone on her bedside table. She reached for the receiver, saw that her hand was trembling and sat down on the bed to compose herself, taking several deep breaths before proceeding to make the needed contact. A few minutes later she was connected to the man who could give her the critical information.

"This is Miranda Wade, manager of the King's Eden Resort."

"Hi, there! What can I do for you?"

"Today we took a booking for a Mr and Mrs Bobby Hewson…"

"Ah yes, made it for him myself. He and his wife had planned to fly on to Broome. Another couple we have staying here—you'll remember them—John and Robyn Trumbell—apparently raved on about King's Eden and they decided to take in a weekend there. Lucky you could accommodate them."

"Yes. Would that be the Bobby Hewson of the Regent Hotel chain?"

"Certainly is," came the dry reply.

Miranda's heart dropped like a stone.

"And his wife is a member of the Parmentier family who owns the Soleil Levant chain," the manager ran on, confirming their identities beyond any possible doubt. "It's her first trip to Australia. Keen to see the sights."

Coincidence...sheer rotten coincidence that they had connected with the Trumbells! And finding available accommodation here! Miranda felt too sick to speak.

"Mr Hewson mentioned that you'd been trained up to a managerial position at the Regent in Sydney. Sounded as though he was interested in finding out how you're dealing with an outback resort."

Bobby *knew* she was here! It wasn't just a trick of fate. He *knew*. John or Robyn Trumbell must have spoken of her. And that was why he was breaking his trip to Broome to come to King's Eden. Nothing to do with *the sights,* though he'd probably played that line to his wife. Bobby Hewson, Miranda knew with stomach-churning certainty, had *her* in his sights!

"I thought it might be him," she forced herself to say through the bitter taste of bile. "Thank you for filling me in."

"Well, I guess you now know what to expect."

"Yes. I do. Thank you again."

She hung up, her mind crawling with scenarios of what she could expect, and every one of them was a nightmare from hell. Tears started welling, tears of miserable frustration at not having escaped the punishment

Bobby Hewson would inevitably deal out to her for having flouted his plans. She remembered only too well her last meeting with him, her eyes cleared of the gullible scales that had blinded her to the man he really was…seeing the totally selfish ego behind his smiling charm.

He had expected her to give in to him.

She'd walked away. Flown away.

And now he was going to catch up with her.

The tears overflowed and trickled down her cheeks. She bent over, pulled off her shoes and socks, then curled up on the bed, hugging a pillow for comfort. She was facing a totally wretched situation. He'd arrive tomorrow, then all day Saturday, all day Sunday, three nights…and he'd be getting at her every chance he had. She knew he would.

Regrets for ever having fallen in love with him savaged her as she wept into the pillow. It hadn't been a real love. More a prolonged affair, sugared and peppered by the excitement and glamour Bobby always brought with him on his flying trips to Sydney. He'd swept in and out of her life, dazzling her with his charm, seducing her with honeyed words, always leaving with the promise of having more time with her on his next visit, making her feel important to him, necessary to him.

She'd fitted in with what he'd wanted. He hadn't cared about her needs. Didn't care about them now, either. He was coming here to satisfy himself, and he'd be scoring off her any way he could…subtle little digs in front of his wife, then seeking her out privately, maybe even trying to get into her bed again. He would see that as a triumph over her bid to put him out of her life. And if she didn't *oblige* him... Miranda shuddered, every instinct telling her no one frustrated Bobby Hewson and got away with it.

A knock on her door broke into the train of misery. She swiped at her tear-sodden face and looked at her watch. It jolted her to see it was a few minutes past five. The current homestead guests were probably back from their day trips and she hadn't been on hand to deal with any requests or problems. The knock meant someone was looking for her.

She scrambled off the bed, grabbed some tissues, rubbed her eyes and cheeks, shoved her feet into sandals, finger smoothed her hair back behind her ears. The knock came again as she struggled to calm herself enough to answer it. Probably Val, she thought, wanting to pass some message on before leaving for the day.

She opened the door and shock hit her again.

Nathan!

"Ah! You're here." He smiled, his eyes warm with pleasure.

Having steeled herself to face responsibility, Miranda was totally undone by Nathan's smile. The steel collapsed and her whole body turned to jelly.

"I was looking for you to give you Sarah's diaries," he went on, holding out the package he was carrying. "Just as well you are here in your private quarters. Makes it easy to put them in a safe place."

Somehow she lifted her hands to take the package. Her gaze dropped to it as her mind tried to change gears, adjusting to Nathan's presence and recalling what she had anticipated...hoped...from it. Except it all felt unreal now, shaky, without substance. She stared down at the diaries—Sarah's diaries—of a life that was in the past.

"Miranda?"

She heard the query but it seemed to come from a long distance. Her past was all too alive, threatening to mess her up again and she didn't know when or where that would stop, now that Bobby had access to her.

"Is there something wrong?"

Wrong...the awful sense of wrongness was so twisted up inside her... Nathan here at the wrong time... Bobby coming to do more wrong...another wave of tears swam into her eyes. She shook her head, too choked to say anything.

"You did say you wanted to read them." The edge in his voice seemed to slice into her heart. "If you've changed your mind..."

She swallowed hard, fighting to order her mind to come up with something that might cover her failure to welcome his company. "I'm sorry, Nathan. I'm not..." Her voice was wobbling. She scooped in a quick breath and forced herself on. "This is bad timing. But thank you for..."

Her chin was forcibly tilted up. The swift action halted her erratic little speech. She was startled into looking at him, though the moisture in her eyes blurred her vision, preventing any clear view of his reaction to her all too obvious distress.

"You've got a problem. Best you use me to talk it over with, Miranda," he stated firmly.

Before she could raise a protest or deter him from

his purpose, he pushed her door wide-open and was steering her around, his arm hugging her shoulders as he walked her to the closest armchair in her sitting area. He set her down in it, retrieved the diaries from her hold, placed them on the bench that divided off the kitchenette, then closed her door, sealing their privacy.

"Now tell me what's upset you."

She shook her head, knowing he had no control over this situation. "It doesn't have anything to do with you, Nathan."

"If it's resort business, Tommy would want me to help, Miranda," he asserted strongly.

Hopelessly agitated by his insistence on getting involved, she pushed herself out of the chair to plead for him to leave her. "It's personal. You can't help. Please…"

"Try me!"

He stood there, a strong mountain of a man, emitting immovable purpose, and Miranda could feel her own will crumpling under his. She didn't know what to do, couldn't see a way of resolving anything. She wasn't aware of her hands fretting at each other, wasn't even aware that her tear ducts were betraying her inner distress again.

Then he was coming at her and suddenly she was enveloped in a warm embrace, her head was pressed onto a broad shoulder, and a hand was stroking her hair.

"It's okay," he murmured comfortingly. "We'll sort it out. A problem is always better shared."

"No, it's not," she cried, even as she passively accepted his physical support, inwardly craving more.

"Trust me." It was more of a command than an appeal. "Sooner or later you'll have to learn to trust me, Miranda. You might as well start now."

She wanted to, but the thought of explaining everything was so daunting, her heart cringed from it. And what if he misunderstood her position? He hadn't lived in Bobby Hewson's world.

"It's not good," she blurted out.

"So what? Who's perfect?"

Anguish splintered her mind. She could no longer find the point of arguing. "It's the man I told you about," she confided in a fearful rush. "Bobby Hewson. He's coming tomorrow. With his wife. And he knows I'm here. He knows."

CHAPTER ELEVEN

TENSION! Being pressed so close to Nathan, Miranda instantly felt it whipping through him, transmitting a stiffening jolt to her shredded nerves. The firm wall of his chest expanded. The hand stroking her hair clenched. The muscular thighs supporting hers tautened to rock-hardness. It seemed for several seconds, he didn't breathe at all. And neither did she!

Sheer panic threw her mind into chaos. What had she done by spilling that information? He'd wanted to know. He'd asked her to trust him. But words spoken couldn't be taken back. If he was thinking badly of her again...

A primitive savagery seized Nathan's mind. *I will not let him have her. I will not let him hurt her. He's a dead man if he so much as touches her!* Then some spark of rationality pulled him back from that violent edge and argued that he had to handle this situation with some finesse. Miranda was not his and only God knew what she felt for the scum who didn't have the decency to leave her alone.

His breath whooshed out, making her scalp tingle with apprehension. The feeling that she was poised on the edge of an abyss with her whole life in the balance made her heart clench with fear. A surge of adrenaline spurred a need to fight for what she wanted. Though she didn't know how she was going to go about it, she lifted her head, ready to face whatever she had to.

"Right!" he snapped, easing away from her, his hands grasping her upper arms to hold her steady.

She braved meeting his eyes, her own completely dry now, and was stunned by the blue blaze of purpose burning from them.

"So he's the cause of your stress. What are you expecting him to do and why, Miranda? Spell it out to me. I'll be able to help you better if I'm aware of all the nuances to this situation."

Relief! Nathan wasn't judging. He was going to listen…to help. Dizzy from the wrangle of emotions still seizing her brain, Miranda took a deep breath to feed some oxygen into her bloodstream, and tried to focus her mind on delivering the salient facts.

Her mouth was dry. She worked some moisture into it and started to outline the problem, her eyes begging his understanding. "The Hewson family own the Regent Hotel chain. They're…they're very rich, influential. I didn't want to continue any kind of relationship with Bobby once I heard he was committed to marrying Celine Parmentier. Her family owns the Soleil Levant hotels. The marriage was going to give Bobby more power. He said I could ride up the ladder with him or…"

The bitter disillusionment of that scene rushed in on her again, the terms Bobby had laid out, ringing with the kind of corrupt promises that had taken her mother down a road that had emptied her heart of all love.

"Or?" Nathan prompted.

She sighed away the dark, grievous memory and pushed on with the deal Bobby had pressed, the revulsion she'd felt reflected in her voice. "If I didn't see sense, I might find my career on shaky ground. If I sought a position elsewhere, a good reference could be withheld."

Nathan frowned. "But it wasn't. My mother said your references were excellent."

"Bobby didn't expect me to leave. He thought he had me. So he didn't bother instructing the manager to withhold the truth about my capabilities, or cast any slur on them."

"So you left without telling him you were going."

"I told no one about applying for this job or getting it. Once I was notified I had it, I packed up my possessions, handed in my resignation and walked out of the Sydney Regent the same day. To all intents and purposes, I disappeared."

"Drastic action," he mused, as though measuring all it meant.

Sensing some criticism of her decisions, and discomforted by it, Miranda broke out of his hold and paced around the two armchairs that faced the television set before turning to confront him again, her hands gesticulating the urgency she'd felt to escape any rebound effect from walking out on Bobby Hewson.

"I wanted a clean break. King's Eden offered me that. It was out of his reach, not connected to people or places he knew. I thought he couldn't get at me here or do me any damage by bad-mouthing me because this was outside the normal hotel trade."

"Get at you?" Nathan picked up sharply, his eyes searing hers with questions.

She flushed, hating the admission she had to make. Her arms instinctively hugged her midriff, holding in the awful vulnerability she felt. "We were together for three years. You don't just forget all that intimate knowledge, Nathan. And he'll use it. I know he will."

The muscles in his face tightened. A wave of disapproval seemed to come at her and it instantly struck a fierce well of resentment. What about him and his two years with Susan? At least she had thought of marriage with Bobby.

"Do you still want him?" he shot at her.

"No!" she flared, throwing out her hands in exasperated denial. "What do you think this is all about? I don't want anything more to do with him. Can't you see that?"

"I see how upset you are by his coming, which suggests to me the relationship is not dead for you. If it were dead, he couldn't get at you, Miranda," he argued tersely.

"You miss the point," she fiercely retorted. "It's not dead for him. And if you think he's going to leave it alone on my say-so..." She shook her head. "My exit from his life told him I wanted out and he's ignoring it. He's deliberately pursuing me, breaking the other plans he'd made the moment he heard where I was. I didn't invite him."

"No, but that doesn't mean you won't want him when he's with you again."

"He's with *his wife!*"

"Miranda, you can say no in your mind." He

walked slowly towards her, his eyes boring into hers. "You said it to me. And you can mean it in your mind, bolstering the no with any number of reasons. I'm not questioning that."

"Then what are you questioning?" she gabbled, feeling the strong male force of him increase as he stepped closer and closer, encompassing her, sending her nerves haywire, stirring all the wild desires she had nursed in the darkness of the nights. It was Nathan she wanted. Not Bobby. And her heart wept that he should think otherwise.

"I think you're worried about what you'll *feel* when he's here...when you're faced with him. Feelings aren't something we can easily govern. What if he draws you into his arms..."

He followed the words with the action, slowly gathering Miranda close to him, but behind the seemingly controlled deliberation in his eyes, she saw the flicker of something that wasn't controlled at all, and it ignited a wild, wanton recklessness in her. Or perhaps the pressure of his body did, the sexuality that seemed to brood from it and clutch at her.

"When you kissed me back, that morning beside the helicopter...were you missing him, Miranda?"

"No. I wasn't thinking of anything. I just..."

"Responded to me."

"Yes." It was barely a hiss of sound. His head was bending to hers and she wanted him to kiss her now, to completely blot Bobby Hewson out of anything between them.

"Then keep remembering this when he comes,

Miranda." A harshness in his voice now, scraped with raw emotion. "Remember how you feel with me."

Then he did kiss her, and it was no exploratory dip to measure her response, no trial for any special element in their tasting of each other. It was full-scale plunder, a kiss of such driving, demanding passion, Miranda was instantly consumed by the explosion of need it ignited. The hot fusion of their mouths was not enough, nowhere near enough, though as they greedily fed on every possible sensation they could find and savour...intoxicating themselves with kiss after kiss, their hands followed their own instinctive path.

Impossible to remember afterwards whether she tore at his clothes or he tore at hers. The undressing was jerky, erratic, urgent, frantic, the compulsion to be rid of everything that came between them almost violent— no stopping it—no wish to pause or think or do anything other than revel in the impact of their bodies fully touching, bare flesh meeting bare flesh, the hot exciting friction of skin against skin, his hands skimming, squeezing her soft curves, her fingers raking the taut musculature that seemed to bristle with masculinity.

She remembered thinking he was a magnificent bull of a man and she wanted to be mated with him, wanted it more than anything she'd wanted in her life, to have the strength of him inside her, to feel him moving with her...this man who called so deeply to the woman she was, whatever else either of them were.

He propelled them to the bed, hauled her onto it, took the dominant position over her, and she automatically arched her body to meet his as he sought entry. His eyes connected with hers...a fierce blaze of desire...fiercely returned...both of them throbbed with an urgency that could not brook any denial.

Her whole body quivered with elation as she felt him push forward, sheathing himself with her moist heat, her inner muscles convulsing around him in bliss, the hard fullness of him opening a passage that pulsed with wild anticipation, wanting all he could give her. She wrapped her legs around him, pressing him on, and the plunge that followed was exquisitely fulfilling, so incredibly deep it felt as though he had entered her womb, an eerie, intimate sensation that spread out in concentric circles, totally captivating in its intensity.

From that moment on, Miranda's whole being was totally focused on the rhythmic ripples set in constant motion by Nathan's powerful thrusting. She was acutely aware of their strengthening infiltration of every cell of her body, the aching sweetness accompanying their invasion, the sense of their building towards a shattering peak, of pleasure becoming too intense to sustain within the space of her being. A time came when she seemed poised on the edge of it and a cry of anguish broke from her throat.

In the very next instant all the torturous tension exploded into a sunburst of glorious ecstasy, and she was floating in some heavenly space, and the man who had brought her there was sharing it with her, cradling her in a hug that kept them bound together as he rolled to one side, removing his weight, yet still enveloping her in a cocoon of strength, caring, protective, possessive.

Their breathing slowed. The thunder of their heartbeats dropped to a barely discernible pulse. The languor that stole over them was seductive...warm, peaceful, enticing a prolonged stay of judgement on what they'd done. It couldn't be examined with words. It had gone beyond words.

Miranda was acutely aware she had never experienced anything like this before…such primitive, compelling passion…yet somehow instinctively right with this man…and being held by him now felt right, too, as though she belonged with him. While it made no rational sense, her mind stood in awe of these feelings, and the longer he held her, the more immersed she became in the blind conviction that they were meant to come together and this was how a man and woman should feel when they did, and she wished she had always known this. Then she could never have been fooled about what it was supposed to be.

Eventually Nathan spoke. He was trailing strands of her hair through his fingers as she lay with her head on his chest. She felt his intake of breath and the words he said were soft but very, very decisive.

"You don't need Bobby Hewson, Miranda."

Bobby? The part of her life he had inhabited felt so minimised she could barely bring it to mind. "No, I don't," she answered fervently.

"I'll be here tomorrow evening to make sure *he* understands you don't need him."

Here? Did Nathan mean in her bed? How would Bobby know—see—the incredible difference of what she felt with Nathan?

"I'll join you and your party of guests for dinner, but I'll come earlier," he said, his voice firm with the plans in his mind.

Miranda struggled past the fuzziness in hers. Nathan

meant to be with her publicly, showing Bobby she was not alone, very much not alone!

"In time for the Happy Hour gathering," Nathan specified.

"Happy Hour!" Miranda jack-knifed out of Nathan's embrace and looked at her watch. It was almost six o'clock. "I've got to get going. I should be out there." A flush of embarrassment poured into her face as she turned to look squarely at him. "This is my job, Nathan."

"Duty calls," he said equably.

She hurtled off the bed and raced into her ensuite bathroom, frantically turning on the taps in the shower, shoving her hair into a plastic cap and stepping under the hot spray before pausing for breath or further thought. Only then did it strike her that Nathan's mind had been locked on Bobby, before and after, and he hadn't said anything about what he felt with her.

What if it had only been a male competitive thing with him?

Instantly her whole body revolted against this thought. Nathan had wanted her before he'd ever known about Bobby. It had nothing to do with Bobby. Nothing! He was purely incidental in their coming together.

It came as another jolt to realise they hadn't used protection. Just as well she was on the pill to keep her cycle regular. And she couldn't see Nathan being a health risk, having recently been in a long monogamous relationship. All the same, there should have been questions asked.

On the other hand, obviously there had been no premeditation by either of them. Which said something about the strength of the attraction between them. The moment Nathan had started kissing her she'd forgotten Bobby, her job, everything. Such a total wipe-out had never happened to her before. Never. It had to mean something special. There was no other explanation for it.

Clean and fresh again, Miranda turned off the taps and quickly towelled herself dry. A nervous energy possessed her as she attended to her hair and make-up. Had Nathan left, having made his arrangements for tomorrow? Did those arrangements mean more than fixing the problem with Bobby?

She wrapped a towel around herself before emerging from the bathroom. Modesty, at this point, seemed rather foolish but she didn't feel comfortable flaunting her naked body with the heat of passion gone, and if Nathan was still in the apartment...this was so *new*. Her mind was torn over how he viewed the intimacy they had just shared. She wanted to be sure.

He was fully dressed and placing the parcel of diaries he'd brought her on the bedside table when she opened the bathroom door. He swung to face her, his gaze making a swift, comprehensive sweep of her appearance.

"Are you all right?" he asked, searching her eyes for any flicker of concern.

"Yes." She offered an ironic smile. "A little stunned."

He nodded. "I didn't think of protection."

Relief surged through her. It might be practical caring but it *was* caring. "I've been on the pill for quite a while. I used to have problems with..." She shrugged, realising she was gabbling and he wouldn't be interested in how heavily and haphazardly she'd menstruated without medication to give her a normal cycle.

He returned her ironic smile. "I'm usually more responsible. I'm not a health risk, Miranda."

"Neither am I."

"Then there's no problem."

Supposedly not for two healthy adult people accepting a simple case of lust gone wild, Miranda thought, needing more from him than this matter-of-fact manner. He started walking towards her and she was once again mesmerised by the overwhelming power of the man, his air of solid self-assurance.

"I'll go now. You have work to do." He put his hand on her shoulder, a light reassuring touch, and dropped a kiss on her forehead. "Just to remind you to keep *us* in the forefront of your mind tomorrow, when Bobby Hewson arrives." His eyes seared hers with the intense recollection of their intimacy. "Expect me at six o'clock. I'll be here to stand by you. Okay?"

"Yes." Was this all it was to him...blotting out Bobby? "Thank you," she added, searching his eyes for more.

He suddenly grinned. "My pleasure."

She watched him leave, too captivated by his presence to move until the door closed behind him. Then conscience pricked her again and she flew to her cupboard, discarding the towel and hastily pulling on clothes.

Nathan's words—*I'll be here to stand by you*—lingered in her mind. Bobby had never done that, not in the supportive sense Nathan meant. Her mother had never had a man she could truly lean on. It was, at least, one good feeling Nathan had left her with, being able to count on him, and Miranda had no doubt he was as good as his word.

But what about when Bobby was gone? Was she to be another Susan in Nathan's life? His ...*pleasure?*

Miranda shied away from these questions. She couldn't deal with them now. She had guests waiting for her. Everything else had to be pushed aside. Tomorrow would come soon enough...Bobby... Nathan...and hopefully some answers she could live with.

CHAPTER TWELVE

IT WAS her job to greet the incoming homestead guests, and greet them she would, but Miranda's stomach was twisted into a painful knot as she watched Bobby Hewson and his new wife arrive.

He alighted from the luggage buggy first, still looking like a sun-king as she had always thought of him—his light brown hair streaked with blonde, his skin gleaming with a perfect golden tan, a dazzling white smile flashing from a face so handsome it was guaranteed to make any woman melt. But it didn't melt Miranda today. It was a strange shaky feeling, seeing him again and knowing the brilliant facade of the man hid a corrupt heart that could never, never be trusted.

"Miranda..." he called, as though the sight of her filled him with delight. "It's a real pleasure to find a familiar face in the great beyond."

His charm washed over her, too, though once it had invariably turned her inside out, dispelling doubts and making her believe he really did love her, that she was truly the light of his life. This time, her mouth didn't automatically flash a responding smile. She had to force it.

"It's a surprise to see you out of the city, Bobby."

He still managed to look city elegant in shorts and sports shirt, colour co-ordinated in navy, red and green,

119

expensive Reeboks on his feet. His tall, gym-trained athletic body carried all clothes well.

"A new challenge always lifts the spirit," he answered, his eyes raking Miranda from head to toe with sexual intent, even as he held out his hand to the woman now stepping out of the buggy.

Inwardly bristling at Bobby's blatant cockiness, Miranda switched her attention to his wife. Her skin was dark olive, making her look quite exotic, dressed as she was in scarlet shorts, a designer T-shirt—white, splashed with an abstract pattern of colourful poppies—and a very chic straw hat with one scarlet poppy artfully placed on the brim. She was also petite, her figure slender, almost boyish, small firm breasts clearly braless.

Miranda, dressed in her usual day uniform of khaki safari shorts and shirt, suddenly felt like a drab Amazon compared to this woman, but she quickly brushed the comparison aside. She was not in competition with Bobby Hewson's wife and never would be.

Keeping her smile in place, she said, "And you must be Celine. Welcome to King's Eden, both of you."

"Thank you. It is amazing, this outback of yours," she lilted at Miranda, her native French tongue giving her English a very attractive accent. "Very much an exciting adventure."

"I hope it continues to be so," Miranda replied, noting that Celine led the way up the path to the verandah, Bobby strolling a step behind. Detaching himself from his wife?

"Did you manage to make all the bookings I phoned through this morning?" Celine asked eagerly.

"Yes, everything has been arranged," Miranda affirmed.

"Even the boat ride down Granny Gorge this afternoon?"

"The guide will be here by the time you've checked into your suite."

She clapped her hands in glee. "I did not want these few hours wasted."

Close up, Celine was younger than Miranda had imagined. She barely looked out of her teens, her pretty face framed by short black hair styled in a pixie cut, and dominated by big dark eyes, aglow with enthusiasm.

"I think I'll give the gorge a miss, Celine," Bobby dropped casually as they mounted the steps to the verandah.

"But I've booked!" she protested, her face petulant with displeasure as she turned to him.

"You can go, pet," he answered indulgently. "I'd like to have a look around the resort. See how it works."

"Business!" She heaved a vexed sigh.

He ignored it, looking over her shoulder at Miranda, his amber eyes gleaming tigerishly. "I'd like a personal tour, Miranda."

With her, he meant, and every fighting instinct rose to the fore. He was not going to get at her. She would not let him. "As you like. I'll call a guide to come and show you what you want to see."

"Come now, Miranda," he cajoled, steering his wife onto the verandah so that he could step up for a direct confrontation, his body language emitting confident demand. "Don't I merit *you* as my guide?"

She tried to construct an apologetic smile. "I'm sorry. I'm not free this afternoon."

"Oh, I'm sure you could delegate your responsibilities."

"This isn't a big city hotel, Bobby, and doesn't run like one," she explained reasonably. "All my staff have very specific responsibilities..."

"And I have a special request which I have no doubt your employers would understand and appreciate," he cut in, his eyes as hard as gold nuggets.

The threat of blackmail had no teeth here, yet the vindictive ego behind it caused her heart to contract. The thought of Nathan standing by her gave her the courage to defy any pressure to fall in with Bobby Hewson's will.

"I can provide a guide," Miranda repeated firmly. "However, if you wish to arrange something with the King family, I believe Nathan King will be here this evening."

And he won't bend to your will, either, she thought with savage satisfaction.

"Ah! So you can leave this business until then, Bobby." Celine jumped in, curling her arm around his and pouting up at him. "I want you with me."

"Well, if it's important to you, pet..." He patted his wife's hand, smiled at her, but there was no smile in the eyes he turned back to Miranda. They glittered with the promise of getting what he wanted, one way or another. "I shall look forward to meeting Nathan King tonight."

"Guests usually gather around the bar from six o'clock onwards for pre-dinner drinks," she informed them, then stood back to make way for the porter, a cheerful American lad who was working his way around Australia. "The Shiralee Suite, Eddie. The key is in the door."

"Yes, ma'am. If you'll follow me, folks."

A Jeep zoomed up to the homestead.

"There's your guide for the gorge trip," Miranda pointed out. "When you're ready…"

"We will not be long," Celine assured her, pulling Bobby with her in her zest to be off sight-seeing.

Miranda watched them follow their luggage inside, thinking Bobby's wife had no idea what she had married. Or maybe she did and was happy to go along with what he gave her anyway. She herself might have remained indefinitely in his charm-web if this marriage hadn't come up. It was a sickening thought.

As it was, her pulse was still galloping from the stressful encounter. She took a deep breath and headed down the path to give instructions to the guide in the Jeep. He could wait inside for the Hewsons. She didn't want to see them again until she had to. Hopefully Nathan would be with her by then.

Nathan…

As the afternoon wore on into early evening, her confidence in his support started wavering. Could she really trust her instincts about the kind of man Nathan was when she'd been so fooled by Bobby for three whole years?

He was different, she argued. He *felt* different. And he didn't emit a glamorous facade. There was nothing ephemeral about him, more solid substance that wasn't going to change. Or was that hope, more than reality?

Bobby could influence and manipulate people. He would not be so blatant in showing Nathan the ruthless dismissal of anything that stood in his way. He would appeal as to a peer who understood how the world really worked, man to man. And he would slyly undermine her credibility, dressing up lies with half-truths, perhaps even suggesting she had slept her way up in the trade.

Would Nathan still take her side against such supposedly confidential and authoritative information? What did he really know of her, apart from the little she'd told him?

Even if he did take her side, how could she be sure he was doing it because he believed her, or because he wanted to keep having sex with her?

And that was the most unsettling thought of all.

CHAPTER THIRTEEN

TEN past six.

And Nathan wasn't here!

Miranda had finished introducing the Hewsons to the other new guests who had arrived before lunch, as well as suffered Bobby's smarmy hug of familiarity as he confided their former professional connection to the group. Her skin was still prickling with revulsion as she escaped his stroking fingers with the excuse of fetching a tray of hors d'oeuvres.

A mistake to have worn this dress. Its shoe-string straps left too much flesh exposed for wandering hands. She'd chosen it because it was a bright lemon colour and she had matching sandals and the outfit had always made her feel upbeat and confident. Tonight she needed all the confidence she could get.

And she had wanted to look good for Nathan!

Was it another mistake to count on him?

She was half-way to the bar to put in a call to the kitchen when she heard a vehicle pulling up outside. Not the sound of one of the resort Jeeps. A more powerful engine. Her heart did a flip and a heady mixture of hope and relief surged through her. It had to be Nathan arriving!

Forgetting the hors d'oeuvres, she did an about-turn and headed for the doors to the front verandah, her pulse skipping erratically. She wanted him. She needed him. Doubts about his motives were momentarily blotted out. The doors in front of her opened automatically to her approach. In a few blurred seconds she was at the head of the steps to the verandah, and there her swiftly moving feet came to a halt.

It *was* him.

He was rounding the bonnet of a Land Cruiser, his big solid frame silhouetted against the sunset. He paused as he caught sight of her waiting to welcome him, and her heart hammered wildly at the strong visual image of him, stamped on the vibrant colours of the outback sky—long horizontal streaks of yellow behind the black spindly trees on the flat horizon, red and purple clouds clustered above them—and this man... this man looking like a lord of it all, whom nature itself was glorifying.

Then he was striding up the path and the very same skin that had crawled at Bobby's touch started tingling as Nathan's electric energy poured towards her. A quiver ran down her thighs. Her toes curled. Her mind throbbed his name over and over...Nathan, Nathan, Nathan...

She didn't hear the doors slide open behind her.

But she heard the voice and the slimy confidence in it as it said, "Ah! Mr King arriving?" and her heart froze as Bobby Hewson stepped up beside her, once again hanging his arm around her shoulders in an insidious claim of ownership, right in front of Nathan!

The shock of it completely paralysed her. She saw Nathan's step slow, his gaze dart from her to Bobby and back to her, and her mind jammed in horror at what he might be reading from Bobby's action.

"Good evening, Miranda," he greeted her coolly as he came to the end of the path.

His coolness jolted her tongue loose. "I expected you earlier, Nathan," she snapped, hating the situation his tardiness had set up.

Suddenly goaded into not caring how it looked, she spun out of Bobby's hug and stepped aside, throwing out one hand in formal introduction. "This is one of our guests, Bobby Hewson...Nathan King. Bobby has expressed a wish to discuss resort business with you, Nathan. If you'll both excuse me, I have other guests to see to."

She left them to it, her whole body seething with furious emotion. Let them have their man-to-man chat, her mind raged. Let Bobby do his worst behind her back. Let Nathan believe whatever he liked of her. She'd steel herself with all the armour she could summon so that neither man could touch her. It was stupid, stupid, stupid, to count on anyone to do right by her! Especially men who just wanted to feather their beds with a woman they fancied.

Terry, one of the waiters, was serving a selection of hors d'oeuvres to the guests. Bobby's wife was gaily chatting to another couple who had been to Granny Gorge that afternoon, displaying no disturbance of mind over her straying husband, not even a questioning glance at Miranda as she rejoined the group. But Celine's gaze did snap to Nathan when Bobby escorted him inside.

"Ooooh...magnifique!" she breathed in girlish awe, and Miranda sourly thought Nathan undoubtedly had the same effect on every woman. He wasn't only special to her.

Nevertheless, despite his drawing the attention of the whole group, it was she he looked at, his gaze boring straight through her defences, shaking her up again, even as she glared back at him, telling herself she wouldn't let him mean anything to her.

Bobby was talking at him in a confidential manner. There was no discernible response on Nathan's face. As they came within easy earshot, Nathan turned to him and said very clearly, "You have the wrong man. This resort is the business of my brother Tommy, and he's happy to leave its management in Miranda's very capable hands."

So Bobby was already trying to go over her head, Miranda surmised, though Nathan *was* the wrong man for that, which meant he'd try Tommy next.

Bobby frowned. "Surely you network."

"As a family, yes. But none of us interfere with each other's areas of special interests." His face took on a hard arrogance as he pre-empted any reply from Bobby. "Though perhaps I should add that the whole family would swing in to protect any of our interests should they be threatened." His gaze cut straight to Miranda. "We look after our own in the Kimberly."

She was instantly thrown into more turmoil. Did he consider her *his?* Was he promising she was safe from Bobby, regardless of anything the man said to anyone?

"You're one of the Kings?" another male guest queried, obviously fascinated by this exchange.

Nathan swung to him with a little smile of acknowledgement. "Yes. Nathan King. The cattle station is my business. And you are...?"

A flurry of introductions and handshakes followed. A keen curiosity about the running of a cattle station prompted several questions at once.

"Well, one requisite is being ready to cope with any emergency," Nathan answered. "This afternoon one of my stockmen was thrown from his horse and it looks as though his back may be broken."

Expressions of dismay and sympathy rippled around the guests. Miranda frowned. Was this the cause of his late arrival? "Calling an ambulance is not an option out here," he went on. "Under instructions from the flying doctor service, we trucked him in to the station airstrip, loaded him into a plane and flew him off to hospital."

"Any news of him yet?" Miranda asked, guilty about her own selfish concerns when one of Nathan's men might well be fighting for his life.

"No." His vivid blue eyes targeted her. "It was five-thirty by the time we had him safely on his way. I've arranged to be called here when information comes in."

"Of course," she said quickly. "Would you like a drink?"

"Yes." He nodded towards the bar. "Shall I help myself?"

The bar attendant was on his way to the group with a tray of cocktails.

"I'll make you whatever drink you'd like," she offered, hoping to have a few private moments with him.

"Thank you," he returned drily, as though no longer expecting anything from her.

Which made Miranda burn with more uncertainties.

As they both moved towards the bar, Celine called, "Bobby, why is it called a cattle station instead of a ranch?"

Miranda silently blessed the claim for her husband's attention.

"Probably because they use huge road-trains, up to fifty metres long, to take the stock to market," someone else answered.

"Yes, and it's best to get off the road if you see one coming," another guest chimed in, proceeding to recount his experience of road-trains, which occupied everyone else's attention.

A lively distraction from the injured stockman, Miranda thought, then reflected that it might have been Nathan thrown from his horse…and how would she have felt then? Even in her current state of violent confusion, he tugged at something vital in her.

"I'm sorry…about the stockman," she blurted. *And for her rude greeting,* though she couldn't bring herself to say it.

"I'm sorry I wasn't here for you on time," he returned quietly, causing her more inner writhing.

"The injured man was more important," she asserted.

"Sometimes there are injuries that aren't so easily visible."

Miranda's heart contracted. Was he talking about her? Himself? Bobby? She shot him a questioning glance as she rounded the bar to serve him. "What would you like?"

His eyes beamed back commanding authority. "I'd like you to seat me at the end of the dinner table with Bobby and Celine Hewson on either side of me. Right now I'll have a whisky. No ice."

She reached for the bottle of whisky, her hands trembling a little, her mind filling with the kind of poison Bobby would pour into Nathan's ear. "Why do you want to be placed there?" she asked, as she managed to pour his drink.

"I'd also like *you* to be seated at the other end of the table, right away from him."

Right away from Nathan, too. She wouldn't be able to hear what was going on between the two men. Which wasn't fair! How could she defend herself? She handed him the glass of whisky, hating the sense of having no control over the situation.

"What if I don't want that?" she challenged.

His eyes glittered with what looked like contempt. "You like him pawing you?"

"No!" she cried, shrivelling under the implication.

"You want to hear how much he still wants you?"

"You know I don't!"

"Do I, Miranda?" He took a sip of his drink, his eyes savagely deriding her contention. "I know nothing of what's gone on between you since he's arrived. All I know is you cut me dead out on the verandah."

"Nothing's *gone on!*" she hissed. "And I was upset by that little tableau Bobby put on for you when you arrived."

"Running away didn't resolve anything."

"Perhaps I wasn't thinking clearly."

"Undoubtedly you weren't. I see his wife is very attractive. Are you jealous?"

"She's welcome to him."

"Then why are you objecting to the seating I've suggested?"

"Because..." Miranda clamped her mouth shut. It was madness trying to fight this. She'd been right when she'd whirled back inside. Let Bobby do his worst. Let Nathan think what he liked. She was better off out of it. "Fine!" she clipped out. "Have it your way! I hope you enjoy your dinner!"

The bar attendant was on his way back. Miranda used him as interference to avoid anything more to do with Nathan as she returned to the guests. *He* strolled back to the group and began chatting up Celine. Well, not exactly chatting up, but answering her very enthusiastic curiosity about him, and Bobby was content to stay in that little circle of charm, waiting to inject his venom when the chance came.

When it was time to usher everyone to the dining table, Miranda didn't have to do any arranging of the seating. Nathan claimed the chair at the foot of the table. Celine grabbed the seat to the right of him. Bobby naturally took the seat to his left. The others chose where they willed, leaving the chair at the head of the table for Miranda, since that was where she had sat at lunch-time.

From that moment on, it seemed to Miranda, Nathan controlled everything. He played the part of a charismatic host to perfection. He was interesting, amusing, witty, extending himself to entertain everyone, the life of the party, all the guests hanging on his words, enjoying having his company, loving every minute of his good-humoured sharing of himself and his expert knowledge of the Kimberly region.

Miranda doubted they even tasted the food they consumed. No one bothered to comment on it. They were too busy lapping up the unique experience Nathan was giving them. Occasionally he referred things to her, forcing her into the conversation, and she had to respond as a good hostess would, but she kept remembering the two dinner parties at the station homestead where he hadn't bothered to put himself out so much, and she resented this performance from him now…lording it over all of them.

It was probably sticking in Bobby's craw that Nathan was the star attraction. But so what? Did that do any good? Was this some male competition to show her he was better value than Bobby was? If this was supposed to *win* her, it was the wrong way of going about it, as far as Miranda was concerned. She would have preferred to have him sitting next to her, giving her some caring attention instead of impressing how great he was on others.

After the main course was cleared from the table, Celine took herself off to the Powder Room. A fresh coat of glossy red lipstick and a respray of perfume for Nathan's benefit, Miranda darkly surmised. One of the other women asked her about a picnic box ordered for tomorrow and the rest of the party started checking their planned activities with each other.

Miranda saw Bobby lean over to murmur something to the man who'd upstaged him all evening. Nathan's face visibly stiffened. His eyes narrowed. Then he leaned over and said something to Bobby that had her former employer straightening up in his chair.

The two men eyed each other in a long, silent duel. More inaudible words were exchanged. Nathan's expression took on a hard, ruthless cast. Whatever was going on between them was not the least bit entertaining, and Miranda had the sickening feeling she was at the centre of it.

Celine returned to her chair.

The call signal of a mobile telephone came from Nathan's shirt pocket. Conversation halted as attention swung to him, the injured stockman coming to mind again.

"Please excuse me," he said, standing up to move away from the table.

He went out on the verandah to take the call.

The sweets course was served, providing a timely distraction. Miranda had lost her appetite for any more food, her stomach too knotted with tension to accept even a spoonful. Whatever antagonism had just been raised and aired between Nathan and Bobby was bound to make the situation worse for her, and she had to get through two more days—and nights—with the Hewsons.

Compliments about the lemon soufflé flowed around the table. Questions were asked about the chef and what other delights could be anticipated from him. Miranda assured them they would be pleased with whatever Roberto prepared but the menu often depended on the guests themselves. She smiled at the couple going fishing tomorrow and suggested they might provide their next dinner.

"Miranda…"

Her heart jumped at Nathan's call. She turned to see him standing at the opened doors to the verandah, emanating an air of authority that was not about to brook opposition.

"May I have a word with you?"

The polite but very public request could not be turned down. "Yes, of course. Please excuse me," she said to the guests as she stood up.

Chaos tore through her again. If Nathan had received bad news he might have to go. Despite her earlier raging, she didn't want him to leave. A trembling started in her legs, and it was difficult to maintain any sense of independent pride as she crossed the room, her mind feverishly fretting over the outcome of this evening's conflicts.

He smoothly engineered her passage out onto the verandah and drew her far enough away from the doors to allow their automatic closing. His grasp on her elbow was firm, warm, and Miranda felt chilled when he dropped it. Had Bobby turned him off her, or had she done that herself? A devastating emptiness yawned inside her.

"The stockman?" she asked, unable to look Nathan in the face.

"The news was good. The spinal cord wasn't damaged."

"I'm glad to hear it."

"That's not why I called you out. Look at me, Miranda."

A steely command.

For a moment, she looked out at the dark shape of his Land Cruiser, remembering her feelings when she'd seen him arrive, silhouetted against the sunset. There had been hope in her heart then. Now despair pressed its dark fingers on her mind. She dredged up some remnants of fighting spirit and turned her gaze to his, expecting nothing good.

His eyes blazed with relentless determination. "You cannot stay here," he stated unequivocally. "I have called Tommy and apprised him of the situation. He'll fly in first thing in the morning."

Alarm streaked through Miranda. What had Bobby said about her? Why was Nathan involving Tommy? Was she being fired from her position? Summarily removed because of another person's word? Though of course it wasn't just another person. It was her previous employer!

"What did you tell Tommy?" she demanded frantically, needing to know what she had to defend herself against.

"Enough to know Hewson is a threat to his business," Nathan answered tersely. "I want you to go in now and pack a bag, ready to leave. I shall keep the Hewsons occupied while you do this."

"But where am I to go?" *What had Bobby said? How was he a threat? And why did she have to leave?* "You can't do this to me," she protested. "Not without telling me why. I'm entitled to an explanation."

"I'm not *doing* anything but safeguarding you and the good name of this resort," he retorted, frowning at her response. "As to where you're going, with me, of course. You can spend the weekend at the station homestead. Once the Hewsons are gone, you'll resume your position here.''

She wasn't being fired! ''I'm to go...*with you?*'' she repeated dazedly.

''Yes. I promise you will be safe with me, Miranda. Is my word good enough for you?''

''Safe...from Bobby, you mean,'' she said, trying to sort through her confusion.

''From me, as well...if that's concerning you,'' he said harshly.

She shook her head, knowing Nathan would not force himself upon her. But to go to such extreme measures...''I want to know what Bobby said. Why you're doing this,'' she cried.

''Later.'' He gestured an impatient dismissal of these concerns. ''Is there anything you need to organise for the guests tonight, before you leave?'' he pressed, assuming her consent to his plans.

The realisation struck she had no choice in the matter. Nathan and Tommy had already made the decisions. ''No,'' she answered slowly, trying to adjust her mind to this entirely new set of circumstances. ''Though I usually check that they're happy with everything before they retire for the night.''

''You can do that before we leave. What about the morning? Breakfast? Activities?''

Her mind raced over possible problems and saw none. ''It's all been scheduled. It should run without a hitch. There'll be a staff member on duty here.''

''Good! Then go and pack what you need. I'll hold the party together. And don't be long about it,

Miranda.'' His eyes flashed contempt. ''I've had enough of the Hewsons to do me a lifetime.''

He hadn't been enjoying himself…

Still in a state of shock over these new developments, Miranda went back inside to follow Nathan's instructions. It took considerable effort to shake her mind free of the dark, tumultuous brooding that had possessed it since his arrival earlier this evening. However, one comforting fact did emerge. Nathan *had* come to stand by her, to protect her. And now he was taking her right out of the nightmare of having to cope with Bobby any longer.

Relief mixed with a sense of humiliation that it had come to this…taking her out…bringing in Tommy… all because of her history with a man she now despised, a past she had done everything to escape from.

Did anyone ever escape from their past? she wondered.

On the other hand, perhaps she was exaggerating her part in whatever was going on. Maybe there was some threat to the resort, competition planned by the Hewson/Parmentier hotel connection. Bobby's request for her to show him how the resort worked might have another more devious motive than just getting her alone with him.

Assuring herself she'd find out soon enough from Nathan, and having reached her room, Miranda pushed herself into thinking of what clothes to take for a weekend at the station homestead. Except it wasn't just a place to go to, a place of refuge from Bobby Hewson.

She would be spending the weekend with Nathan…in his home.

Safe, he'd said, and his word could be trusted. Miranda didn't doubt that. The problem was…could she trust herself to keep safe from him? She hated the distance she had put between them tonight. Maybe it was a sensible distance. Maybe he no longer wanted to cross it.

What had Bobby said about her?

Her heart quivered in trepidation. Her life didn't feel her own any more. But she went through the motions of packing a bag. A weekend with Nathan should sort out something, she argued. Safe or not, it had to be better than staying here with Bobby Hewson.

CHAPTER FOURTEEN

NATHAN had taken her chair at the head of the table, continuing his assumed role of host in her absence. Miranda noted he was still promoting a congenial mood amongst the guests, though keeping a physical distance from the Hewsons. She dropped her bag near the doors and crossed the lounge area to the split-level dining section, nervously wondering how he intended to direct their departure.

He rose from her chair, pushing it right back so he could gather her to his side, smiling at her as he slid his arm around her waist, deliberately coupling them to face the table guests together.

"All ready?" he asked, his eyes commanding her assent.

"Yes," she murmured, acutely aware of his hand resting possessively on the curve of her hip.

He transferred his smile to the guests who were all watching this linking with speculative interest. "I must beg you to excuse us from the rest of this evening's dinner party," he said charmingly. "Duty calls me back to the station and this is Miranda's weekend off. I've persuaded her to find out firsthand what the life of a cattleman is like."

He turned an intimate grin to her and added, "I can't, in all conscience, expect her to marry me until she knows what she's committing herself to."

Marry!

Miranda was too poleaxed to say a word. Somehow she managed to maintain the smile she'd pasted on her face.

One of the male guests laughingly remarked, "Well, that's making your intentions clear, Nathan."

"One of the things we learn in the outback is always seize the day," he answered good-humouredly. "And when a woman like Miranda comes along, a man would be a fool not to."

Heat bloomed in her cheeks. She rolled her eyes at Nathan, not knowing where else to look. It amused the guests who were obviously enjoying his very open confidences.

"My brother, Tommy, will be here in the morning to manage you through the rest of the weekend," he went on. "Staff will be standing by to see you off on your activities tomorrow. Is there anything you need to check with Miranda before I sweep her away with me?"

The inquiry brought only jovial remarks.

"We're all set. Best of luck to you, Nathan!"

"Yo! We've made a note of everything. Got to say you two look well-matched."

"No problem for us. Don't let him steam-roller you, Miranda."

"Huh! Firsthand knowledge sounds good to me!"

"I would seize the night if I were you, Miranda," Celine said archly.

Everyone laughed.

Except Bobby, who remained silent. Miranda didn't look at him, but she was extremely conscious of his presence and his lack of response. This performance by Nathan was for *his* benefit. She hoped it was having the right effect, whatever that was supposed to be.

Marry!

Nathan couldn't mean it. Why go so far? *What had Bobby said to him?*

"Then we'll say goodnight to you. Enjoy yourselves." Nathan rolled on, saluting them with one hand and digging the fingers of the other into her hip to prompt her into appropriate speech.

"Have a great time, all of you!" she rushed out. "And thank you for your good advice. It's a bit hard to catch one's breath around Nathan."

It left them laughing.

They didn't know how true it was.

All the way out to his Land Cruiser, Miranda was in a ferment over his words and actions. His arm remained lodged around her waist, and she could feel his determination to prevent any backward sliding from his stated plan. It wasn't desire for her company driving him. He had taken control and was relentlessly pushing through what he considered had to be done.

He opened the front passenger door and half-lifted her into the high seat. Her bag was stowed on the bench seat behind her. There was no time wasted in putting himself behind the steering wheel and getting the Land Cruiser into motion. His face was grim as they sped away from the resort homestead, and Miranda had to take a very deep breath to combat the throat-strangling tension he emitted.

"What did Bobby Hewson say to you?"

Jaw-clenching silence.

Her heart cramped at this evidence of damage done, but she could not let the issue rest any longer. "This is *later*, Nathan. I'm entitled to know."

"He was surprised you had been hired for such a position of trust without a thorough investigation into your background," he answered, his voice grating out the words.

Miranda clenched her hands at the implication she could not be trusted. "In all my working life, I have never once been considered unreliable. Your mother saw my references," she shot at him.

"He proceeded to tell me *your* mother was little better than a whore, a kept mistress who'd serviced several married men, one of whom had fathered you. She'd also been an alcoholic who eventually drank herself to death."

The stark facts of her mother's life sounded ghastly, stripped as they were of any mitigating circumstances or sympathetic understanding. Miranda felt sick, remembering how Bobby had wanted to know more about her life and had been sweetly comforting when she had confided the truth. But she had never, never used such brutal terms in speaking of her mother, and she had wept over the sadness of it all...the initial deceit of a married lover who had left her alone and pregnant, the inability to cope and the desperate drowning of that inability in alcohol.

She closed her eyes, savagely berating herself for having revealed such deeply personal matters to a man who had no compunction in using them against her. Pillow-talk. Intimacy she had believed was precious to both of them. Now this malicious betrayal of it.

"Did he tell you I was bent the same way?" she asked dully.

"He said you knew how to work the sexual angles to your advantage, that he himself had been pleasured by you in years gone by, and he wouldn't put it past you to fleece any male guest who fancied you."

Humiliation burned her soul. "It's not true," she whispered. "I've never...*sold* myself. He's saying these things because he thought he could buy me and I wouldn't go along with it."

"You don't have to defend yourself to me, Miranda. I don't enjoy repeating this muck-raking. It was all I could do, not to smash his face in."

Relief poured some soothing balm on her wounds. At least Nathan believed she was being slandered. In fact, the sheer savagery in his voice spurred the courage to open her eyes and really look at him. His face was taut with barely suppressed anger. His knuckles gleamed almost white where he was gripping the steering wheel.

"You had to be taken out of there," he said with biting conviction. "He would have used you to create a nasty situation. He was setting up for it. Without you as a flesh-and-blood focus, he loses his teeth. In moving you onto my ground, there's no way he can get at you."

Miranda sighed, understanding his tactics and grateful for being spared Bobby's treacherous company, but suspecting frustration would only drive the slandering further. "It won't stop him telling lies about me, Nathan. In fact, your suggestion of marriage will probably fuel his claim of my playing the sexual angles for profit.''

"No. It reinforces how serious my threat was to him.''

"Threat?'' The idea startled her. Then she remembered the hard, ruthless cast of his face when he had answered Bobby at the dinner table. "What did you threaten him with?'' she asked, unable to think of anything that would hurt a Hewson.

"I told him if I heard so much as another word breathed against you, I would set about wrecking his marriage and the Hewson-Parmentier merger with every bit of armament at my disposal.''

Shock pummelled her. "But how could you do it?''

"Through his wife.''

"You would hurt her?''

"Against him I would use anything.'' He slanted her a hard, cynical look. "Don't be wasting your sympathy on the sultry Celine…a new bride, fancying a lustful dalliance with me. Hardly an expression of true love for her husband.''

It was all very well to criticise the morality of others, but if Nathan had been encouraging Celine, was he any better? Feeling very much at odds with this tactic, Miranda recalled his reaction to her own supposed position of mistress to a married man. "You told me adultery wasn't your scene,'' she tersely reminded him.

"It's not,'' he replied without hesitation, shooting her a sardonic look as he added, "but neither of them know that. I'm bluffing, Miranda, and a bluff only succeeds if it is credible.''

"Do you think it's credible...talking about marrying me?"

"There wasn't a person around that table who didn't believe me," he said with arrogant confidence.

A bluff...Miranda closed her eyes again, a dull weariness settling through her. Right now it was all too much...Bobby's mean and malevolent assault on her reputation, Nathan's moves to counter it. Though, of course, he did have to counter it—Tommy, as well— or the slurs on her character could very well taint the good name of the resort, most especially with the wealthy guests who invariably passed on good or bad word of mouth to their friends.

"You'd better warn Tommy that you talked about marrying me," she said tiredly. "The guests might bring it up with him."

"I've told him. He'll play along."

"They might chat with others on the resort, too. The guides...Sam..."

"A pleasant piece of gossip doesn't matter. And I made it clear it was me pursuing you, Miranda, not the other way around," he added drily.

"And eventually I'm to decide not to marry you."

He expelled a long breath. "As I've said before, most women wouldn't choose my kind of life."

"Is that what happened with Susan?"

The words slipped out, probably because she was too stressed to monitor what she said, though she didn't regret the intrusion into his private background, justifying it on the grounds that he knew all of hers now. Why not get the truth out in the open? Then maybe she could get a fix on where she actually stood with

Nathan, instead of feeling as though she was caught in another web of deceit.

"No," he answered slowly. "Marriage was never on the cards with Susan."

"You just had a mutual sex thing going," Miranda muttered bitterly, having been all too freshly reminded of how Bobby Hewson had used her.

"I suppose you could put it that way, though we were also friends and I always enjoyed her company," he said quietly. "Because of injuries from a car accident in her teens, Susan couldn't have children. She told me straight up not to ever get seriously attached to her. It was her unshakable belief that one day I would want children of my own and she'd hate not being able to give them to me."

Had he tried to shake that belief? Out of a whirl of confusion came one definite fact. "Sam told me she did marry."

"Yes. To a widower who already had two young children. Susan is a schoolteacher. One of the children was in her kindergarten class last year. She told me it was her chance to be a mother and she was taking it. I was not prepared to argue that, Miranda. It was her choice."

Never judge anything before hearing all the circumstances, Miranda silently berated herself, shamed by the full story of Nathan's relationship with the woman who had engaged his interest for two years. He hadn't said he'd loved Susan but there'd been caring in his voice, caring for her personally and respect for the needs he couldn't answer.

There had to have been a sense of loss when she'd

chosen the widower with the children, closing Nathan out of her life. The ending of any long relationship left an empty place. Even Bobby's defection had left her ravaged. For Nathan it would have been much worse, presented with a set of circumstances he couldn't fight, forced to let go by his own code of decency. And since then, he'd been alone for months, Sam had told her, not interested in picking up with anyone else.

Until she had arrived on the scene and a strong sexual chemistry had hit both of them.

Had it been that way between him and Susan?

Impossible to ask. It was wrong to make comparisons. People were different and their relationships were different. She darted a glance at him but his expression was closed to her, his concentration fixed on the road. It startled her to see they were driving through the station's community, almost at the homestead.

"I'm sorry," she blurted out. "I shouldn't have brought up Susan like that."

He shrugged. "It was on your mind."

He brought the Land Cruiser to a halt in front of the entrance to his homestead and switched off the engine. For a few moments he sat frowning, his fingers tapping the steering wheel. Then he turned to her with a look that was searing in its intensity.

"I'm not another Bobby Hewson, Miranda. I have never acted dishonourably over any woman and never would. I don't want you coming into my home, feeling at risk in any way. If you do feel...compromised in some fashion...I'll take you somewhere else...to one of the families on the station..."

"No. This is fine," she protested in an agony of

embarrassment at her own blind and bitter thoughts about him. "I do trust you, Nathan. God knows you've proved you're a decent person and I thank you, very sincerely, for all the trouble you've gone to on my behalf."

He nodded, his eyes still burning into hers, intent on scouring any doubts. "I'll put you in a guest suite. I think it best if you accompany me out on the station tomorrow. Can you be up, dressed and ready for breakfast by six-thirty in the morning?"

She was too drained to argue anything any more. "If there's an alarm clock in my room and it works."

"I'll set it for you."

Decisions firmly made, he alighted from the Land Cruiser, collected her bag and was opening her door before Miranda could collect wits enough to get out of the vehicle by herself. "Thanks," she murmured as he steadied her wobbly step onto the ground.

"Want to hang onto my arm?" he offered kindly.

"I'm okay. Just tired."

Too tired to even try to figure out what Nathan was feeling, how he saw her now. There were so many layers to him...kind, caring, ruthless in carrying through decisive action, shouldering responsibility at a moment's notice, a masterful controller of situations, yet still respectful of others' choices.

Part of her very much wanted to hang onto him. Part of her recoiled from giving him any reason to wonder if she was the kind of woman Bobby Hewson had painted...perhaps giving him sex yesterday so he would take her side today.

Though it hadn't been like that.

She hoped Nathan realised it had been some spontaneous need, triggered by the man he was, nothing else. Nevertheless, she could hardly blame him for wondering about it. If enough dirt was thrown, some of it stuck, and Bobby had certainly done his worst to hang dirt on her tonight.

Too sensitive on this point to touch Nathan even accidentally, Miranda kept a safe space between them as she accompanied him inside, down the long central hallway to another hall that ran at right angles to it. They turned into this and halfway along he opened a door, switched on a light and stood back, waving her ahead of him.

It was a very welcoming room, a pretty patchwork quilt on an old-fashioned brass bed, richly polished cedar wardrobes and chests of drawers giving a warm character to the rest of the furnishings. Following her in, Nathan placed her bag on the end of the bed and moved straight to the lamp table near the bedhead, indicating the clock radio there.

"Will five-thirty give you enough time?" he asked.

"Yes. Thank you."

He set the alarm, then pointed out the door between the two wardrobes. "Your ensuite bathroom is through there. Would you like me to fetch you a hot drink or..."

"No. I just want to drop into bed. Thanks for looking after me, Nathan. I'm sorry I've brought this trouble..."

"It's not your doing," he cut in emphatically. "Just put Hewson behind you, Miranda. You won't see him again, I promise you."

Seeing Bobby again was not really the problem. As she watched Nathan give her a wide berth as he moved towards the door, she suddenly couldn't bear the thought that tonight's nasty insinuations were simmering away in his mind, seeding doubts about her integrity.

"Nathan…"

The needful cry halted him. His shoulders squared before he turned around, and she mentally cringed at what seemed like his reluctance to face her again. He looked back at her with hooded eyes, tensely waiting for her to complete whatever she wanted to say.

Only her deeply ingrained sense of self-worth drove her on, her eyes begging his belief. "I've never used sex to—" she agonised over the right words, desperate to correct the impression he might have "—as a tool to gain some advantage for myself."

"Miranda, if that was the way you worked, you would have targeted Tommy," he said with quiet conviction. "Don't fret over what we might think. Neither Tommy nor I will be shaken from what we've seen of you and how you've conducted yourself since you've been at King's Eden."

Tears pricked her eyes.

"You have earned the right to our support and protection," he went on. "So rest easy tonight, knowing you have it and we won't fail you."

She nodded, too choked up to speak. No one had ever thrown support behind her like this, such an unstinting degree of faith and loyalty. It gave her almost a sense of belonging, as though she was accepted as *one of their own.*

Nathan moved back to where she'd stayed, near the bag at the foot of the bed, and gently touched her cheek. "It must have been rough, growing up in such an insecure environment," he murmured sympathetically. "I admire what you've made of yourself, Miranda. It shows a lot of grit...a strong drive for survival. Don't let that slimy bastard beat you down now because you're worth a million of him. He's glitter and you're gold. Believe me...I know."

His hand dropped to her shoulder and he gave it a light squeeze. "Tomorrow is another day. Okay?"

"Yes," she managed huskily.

His mouth curved into an ironic little smile. "Who knows? We might even make a go of marriage, you and I."

He left her with that thought. Miranda had no idea if he was even remotely serious but just the idea of the possibility served to lift a cold, leaden weight off her heart. She touched her cheek where he had touched it, treasuring the lingering sense of warmth. It felt good.

And tomorrow was another day.

CHAPTER FIFTEEN

MIRANDA had no trouble putting Bobby Hewson behind her the next day. She was literally transported to another world. From the safety of Nathan's helicopter, she watched in awe at the incredible skill of the pilots in the two bubble helicopters, swooping from side to side as they flushed cattle out from under scrubby trees and drove them from watercourses, the clatter of the blades and the roar of the motors relentlessly pressing them into a mob and moving them towards a stock-camp.

On the ground, fences were cut in front of the gathering herd as it was funnelled from paddock to paddock and the numbers kept swelling. By lunch-time several hundred head of cattle had been mustered and driven halfway to the holding yards, where the weaned calves were to be branded and the stock for sale selected.

Nathan had informed her over breakfast that the station ran about thirty-six thousand head of cattle, and six thousand were trucked away each year. The breeding program he'd instigated more than made up these numbers. In different parts of the station were Brahman and English Shorthorn breeds, but these were Africanders, handsome red beasts who could thrive in the most arid areas.

Their movement and colour looked stunning on the backdrop of the vast, beige Mitchell grass plains. There was a wild element to the mustering that added the

thrill of danger, a pitting of man against the challenge
of the landscape and the unpredictability of cattle that
were used to going where they willed, yet there was
also a marvellous orchestration to it—the men and machines on the ground supporting the men and machines
in the air, gradually dominating a long practiced strat-
egy against the seemingly indomitable.

This was what Nathan's life was about, Miranda
realised, and the grand sweep of it deeply impressed
her; the understanding of how it worked, the skill and
experience at controlling what was controllable, the
management of time and place, and at the heart of it,
an environment that demanded an intimate knowledge
of its unique natural harmony.

They had lunch by the river, close to where drums
of fuel had been set up for the helicopters. Nathan was
clearly at ease with his stockmen, welcomed into their
company, Miranda accepted without any fuss. A fire
had been lit and a billy of water put on to make tea.
They sat under the shade of trees and ate damper and
slabs of cold meat, the men chatting over the morning's
progress, Miranda content to simply immerse herself in
the sights and sounds around her.

Here on the ground she could hear the thunder of
hooves and the bellowing of the cattle. She could taste
and smell the dust of the mob, and watch the tight
intricate ballet of the mustering helicopters. Somehow
it made life very vivid, real and earthy in a bigger sense
than Miranda had ever experienced before. It was
strangely intoxicating as though something heady had
seeped into her bloodstream.

The heat of the day added a shimmering haze to the

light and when Nathan stood up, marking the end of their lunch-break, an aura seemed to gleam from him, lending even more stature to the man. He turned his gaze to her and the blue magnets of his eyes drew on her soul as though he was willing her to be bonded with him and in more than a physical sense.

His outback empire was both harsh and beautiful and she had the strong feeling he was asking if she could be part of it, if she could accept it and live with it as he did...and she knew in that instant there was nowhere for them to go unless she could honestly say *yes*. Impossible to make a marriage on sexual attraction alone, if marriage really was on his mind. It was this land that had first claim on Nathan—always would— and if she couldn't share it with him, she lost what truly made him what he was.

A subtle challenge rang through his voice as he said, "Time to move on," and held out a hand to pull her up onto her feet.

He didn't ask her if she was tired, if she'd prefer to stay at the camp by the river. Taking his hand symbolised her willingness to be where he was, see what he saw, learn the enduring pattern of his life firsthand and judge if she could fit into it. Miranda understood this intuitively, yet the feel of his hand enveloping hers was far more immediate, stimulating a strong awareness of the sexuality zinging through their physical togetherness.

He kept possession of her hand as they walked back to his helicopter and Miranda felt like dancing, her heart was so joyously lightened by the prolonged link. Nathan hadn't exactly been distant towards her since last night but his manner had remained strictly on a friendly, matter-of-fact level, which she had found inhibiting.

It was almost as though he was denying they had ever shared any intimacy and she hadn't been sure if this was to reassure her of no sexual pressure intended this weekend, or if he was reserving judgement on there being any possible future in their relationship.

There would be no false promises from Nathan King. Miranda had no doubts on that score. But his hand said he did want her and that hadn't changed. She couldn't resist moving her fingers slightly, savouring the touch of rough skin and warm strength, craving the solidity of all this man emitted.

He shot her a questing glance. "You were quiet over lunch."

"I had nothing to contribute."

"You could have asked questions."

"I didn't want to intrude."

"I don't want you to feel like an intruder, Miranda."

"I don't. I just wanted to listen, to take everything in."

"So what did you think?" His eyes were more intensely probing this time.

"I think that any woman who wanted to separate you from all this would have to be deaf, dumb and blind not to realise you *are* this and inseparable from it."

He gave her a funny little smile, something between wry acknowledgement and self-mocking resignation. "Do you find that off-putting?"

"No. It makes me want to know it all, Nathan," she answered with absolute sincerity.

Another sharp glance, then a long expulsion of breath. When he spoke, his voice was dry and flat. "Well, when your curiosity turns to boredom, I guess I'll know. I've had plenty of practice at recognising the signs."

She had no answer to the deeply rooted scepticism seeded by previous women in his life. Only time could lend truth to whatever she felt about him...now or years from now. Yet in her heart, Miranda was certain she would never be bored with Nathan King. There was something so special in the essence of the man, she couldn't imagine its ever losing its hold on her.

And this outback world had its hold, too. At the end of the day, a thousand head of wild cattle from three huge paddocks had been mustered into stockyards and the helicopters headed for home, their flying insect-like shapes silhouetted against the red flares of the sunset. They flew over what seemed like kilometres of nothing in the gathering darkness, yet Miranda was aware this was deceptive, that life was more spaced out here than anywhere else and it moved to a beat of its own.

Then in the distant landscape there appeared pin-pricks of light, a cluster of them, and Miranda's heart lifted with a sense of homecoming as she realised they were the lights of the station buildings being switched on. It was strange...feeling they were welcoming her, like a friendly beacon drawing her in to a safe harbour. Lights had never had that effect before. Somehow, between yesterday and today, it seemed more shifts had taken place in her life.

Or perhaps it simply represented the kind of home she yearned for, a place of belonging, light after dark, a long, solid reality that lasted, regardless of good times and bad, a core history of humanity that had stayed, survived, prospered, and was now embodied in Nathan who had brought her into it with such protective caring. Safety, comfort, love…

Could he love her?

The question remained almost feverishly in her mind as they returned to the homestead, then parted to wash and change into fresh clothes for dinner. Showering made her intensely conscious of her body, how it had fitted to Nathan's, how it had felt, and it was difficult to push those memories aside and concentrate on what Nathan would want from her in the long term. Sex was not enough. Yet even sternly telling herself this did nothing to lessen her state of arousal.

The need for him continued to course through her. She put on a soft wraparound dress—a little black dress that was meant to be worn braless—knowing it would make her look accessible, wanting him to know she was accessible to anything he offered her. That was the raw, bottomline truth and she wasn't going to flinch from it any more or let any fear of consequences get in the way.

When they met in the lounge room for pre-dinner drinks, she could barely stop herself from eating him up with her eyes, the sheer maleness of his magnificent physique hitting her anew. Her pulse was galloping as he handed her a glass but his fingers didn't touch hers and he took a seat away from her, signalling his intent to control whatever he felt.

Miranda wished *she* could. Reason finally came to the fore, prompting her to ply him with questions about how the station worked, the various responsibilities of the people he employed, the schedule everyone followed to accomplish what had to be accomplished. The mental challenge of taking in his replies and fitting them all together was stimulating, too.

Not once did the conversation lag over dinner. Miranda was frightened to let it because she knew any silence would fill with sexual tension and he might think this was all there was between them. She was hungry for much, much more. All of him, not just the body that called so strongly to hers.

As it was, her interest in his world acted as an aphrodisiac, because his answers filled out the kind of man he was and to Miranda he was everything a man should be, very hands-on in taking care of every part of his business, treating his people with integrity and respect, aiming for the best that could be done within the parameters of what he worked with.

After dinner he took her to his office, pressed into showing her the map of King's Eden, pointing out the location of the different breeds of cattle and how they would be mustered over the coming month, giving her a visual picture of the whole operation and a better understanding of the scale of it. To her captivated heart and mind, it was a kingdom, and it could be an Eden...with Nathan.

He was explaining more to her but she lost the thread of what he was saying, her gaze fastening on his pointing hand, running up his tautly muscled arm, over his broad shoulder to the strong brown neck laid bare by the opened collar of his shirt. She didn't hear his voice trail into silence. Her ears were filled with the drum of her own heart as she saw the pulse at the base of his throat move to the beat of his.

Slowly his chest turned towards her and the hand that had been pointing drew back and curled over her shoulder, pulling her around to face him squarely. Realising she had been caught being inattentive, Miranda lifted pleading eyes to his, a flush of guilt scorching her cheeks as she cried, "I'm not bored. I..."

Her mouth dried up under the searing look of hunger that burned with all the urgent heat of her own. He lifted his other hand and with featherlight fingertips stroked a few wayward strands of hair from her brow, then the soft skin at the corner of her eye, her cheek, her lips, a fine tingling tracery that stirred every nerve-ending into exquisite anticipation and caught the breath in her throat.

But he didn't kiss her. His eyes didn't move from hers. Only his hands moved, a sensual caress of her neck, shoulders, softly hooking the supporting straps of her dress with his thumbs and slowly pulling them down her arms, the cross-over pattern of the bodice parting, opening wide, sliding down the slopes of her breasts, caught briefly on peaks that had hardened with tremulous excitement before dropping to her waist, baring her breasts.

Yet still his gaze held hers, the naked hunger simmering into a lustful challenge that demanded her consent to the charged desire driving his fingertips to savour every tactile sensation, the silky texture of her skin, the curve of her spine, swirling patterns of touch all over her back, her arms, arousing erogenous zones she never knew she had, the side swells of her breasts,

the hollow below her rib-cage, then upwards, circling
her aureoles, outwards and inwards, building a delicate
web of sensual intensity that was utterly captivating.

Then his palms, softly rotating nipples that were begging for attention, and a flare of exultant pleasure in
his eyes as he saw the sweetly relieving pleasure of it
in hers. No rush to passion tonight. The wanting had
been mounting all day, and the desire to satisfy every
bit of it was a consensual current neither of them could
deny now.

She undid the tie at her waist and the soft fabric of
her dress slithered to the floor. The stretch lace briefs
she wore provided the smallest barrier to complete nakedness yet she felt no self-consciousness about her
body. Nathan wasn't even looking at it. He was touching her mind, wordlessly telling her he had craved feeling her like this, revelling in the full sensation of her
femininity, determined on missing nothing, wanting her
to feel him wanting all of her.

The need to reach out to him in like manner drove
her hands to feel for the lowest button on his shirt. A
wild glitter leapt into his eyes, then was forcibly tamed.
"Later if you want," he said gruffly, "but this I must
have first."

Miranda found herself swept off her feet before she
could begin to read his intention. In a few breathless
seconds he carried her from the office by way of a
connecting door to a bedroom she had to assume was
his. The bed he laid her on was wide and long, king-
size, the head of it piled with thick pillows, the rest of
it covered with a softly padded quilt. The only light
was from the opened doorway so there was no seeing

any detail even if she'd been interested in looking. At this heart-pounding moment anything beyond Nathan was irrelevant.

He removed her briefs and sandals, his hands caressing her legs, her feet, sensitising every area he touched, leaving her flesh humming with excitement. Then he stood back and undressed himself, but not once did his gaze leave her, his clothes being discarded with methodical purpose while he spoke in a low, thrumming voice that wound around her and held her tied to him.

"Countless times have I envisaged this...you lying here on my bed, waiting for me, wanting me, nothing between us but the time it takes to come together. I don't know why it's so. It just is. Like a compelling need I cannot put aside."

"Yes," she whispered, her throat tightening at the sight of his nakedness emerging, what it meant to her, what it could mean if he shared what she felt. Need...yes...but did it go beyond what he'd known with any other woman?

Please let it be so, she fiercely prayed.

He spoke again, seeming to answer her prayer. "That first evening, when you walked into my life...it was like...this woman was made for me...no sense to it...sheer instinct beating it out. And every time I see you, the same message clamours through me, regardless..."

Regardless of what? she wanted to ask, but he leaned over and claimed her mouth in a long ravishing kiss that splintered any coherent thought. She felt him stretch out beside her, one tautly muscled thigh inserting itself between hers, a hand cupping her breast, gently kneading it as his mouth devoured hers with more and more erotic passion.

"Made for me," he breathed against her lips, a husky claim, reinforced by his hand gliding down over her stomach, fingers weaving through the silky curls at the apex of her thighs, stroking intimately, making her gasp as he aroused an explosion of exquisite yearning.

"Do you know how much I want to make you mine?" he murmured, trailing hot kisses down her throat. "To taste you, to take you inside me, to be inside you…"

How could she think…answer…the questions were being swamped by feeling.

His mouth closed over her breast, drawing it into a wild rhythmic threshing that was suddenly echoed by a more invasive stroking, a circling of her vagina, an internal caress, a teasing tantalising slide and glide that had her arching for more.

He moved his mouth to her other breast, sucking harder, tugging in a crescendo of possession given and taken as she writhed to the intense pleasure of his knowing touch, mindless to anything but the fantastic sensations arcing through her. She cried out an anguished protest when he withdrew from her, heaving himself down to the foot of the bed, but almost instantly he forged an even more intimate connection, kissing her as deeply there as he had her mouth, his lips covering other pleasure-swollen lips, his tongue seeking a sweeter cavern.

A fiercer pleasure screamed through her, driving her frantic as she felt the tension of it build towards the flood of climax. "No...no...I want you...you..." she sobbed, hands grabbing his hair, pulling hard.

He rose like a dark force of shimmering energy and surged into her, filling the need and rocketing her into the first convulsive wave of ecstatic satisfaction. Her legs whipped around him, holding him deep within, exulting in the sweet tidal flow he had set in motion.

But he didn't drive it on as she expected. He maintained the full union with her, letting the awareness of it throb acutely through both of them as he propped his body over hers, his chest brushing the extended peaks of her breasts, his eyes blazing into hers with a furnace of feeling.

"Does this feel special to you, Miranda? More special than anything you've ever known?"

The question seized her mind, focused it, forced a deeply primitive retaliation. "Is it to you?"

"Would I ask if it wasn't? I want to know if what I feel is echoed in you and I need the truth."

In a sudden flash, she realised it was Bobby disturbing Nathan's trust in her response to him, Bobby who had stirred too many bad feelings for either of them to dismiss easily. Yet he didn't belong in this precious moment. He might have been the catalyst that had driven them to this acknowledgement of each other, but the truth was...Bobby Hewson was nothing and Nathan was everything.

Her eyes met the fire in his with all the open honesty he was now giving her, the answers she'd craved...and the rightness of it poured a blissful conviction into her voice as she answered him.

"It's been the same for me...all you said...from

when I first saw you." She lifted her hands to his face, cupping it, pressing her need for possession of him as she added, "I don't care if it makes sense or not. If I could have a man made for me, it would be you."

"No ifs, Miranda. I'm here with you, in you *now*. Am I the man for you?"

"Yes." The answer came unequivocally. "All that you are, Nathan."

"Then show me."

His arms burrowed under her and he rolled, turning onto his back and carrying her so she straddled him, still with the hard fullness of him inside her, waiting for her to go beyond passive acceptance, to be as positive in action as her words had been. He was giving her the freedom to express her desire, her need for him, and the surprise spurred by his challenge of mutuality swiftly zoomed into elation.

It wasn't a matter of showing him anything. She wanted to touch him, to caress and excite and tantalise and arouse him to the same incredible pitch of pleasure that would rip all control apart and plunge them both into the same beautiful sea of ecstatic release.

She tasted, licked, kissed, stroked, wherever desire took her, all the time consciously keeping him inside her, voluptuously rolling around him, sliding forward and backwards, feeling every inch of him enveloped and squeezed, released and teased. It was a glorious, glorious feeling...Nathan, all hers.

She exulted when she heard him catch his breath, when she felt the flesh under his skin quiver, when a husky growl escaped from his throat. Her own pleasure continued to come in delicious waves with the movement she manipulated herself, but the best of it came when he could stand no more of being *taken*.

He erupted into action, heaving her back onto the pillows, gathering her to him, plunging himself hard and fast as though his survival depended upon it, a violent, primitive mating, his energy pouring into her in bursts of need—*compelling* need—no other woman made for him—not like her—none like her—and she was drawing this from him, climbing with him until they both reached a peak of fierce jubilation in their ultimate togetherness.

They hugged each other tightly, wanting the oneness to go on and on...the reality of it, the sense of it, the flow of feeling...and for a long, long time they shared the blissful harmony. Miranda was drifting into drowsiness when Nathan spoke, his voice humming softly in her ear.

"Is it too soon to hope you will be my mistress, Miranda?"

Her heart instantly contracted at his use of a word that had so many painful memories attached to it. She could barely bring herself to speak, but reason insisted he had to be thinking in more than sexual terms. Or was her own need for more than a sexual relationship colouring reason?

"What do you mean?" she asked flatly, trying to keep her emotions in check.

He wound a long tress of her hair around his hand, then let the silky strands of it slide through his fingers. "Is this ephemeral, or something we can keep?" His chest rose and fell as he expelled a long sigh. "I'm asking if there's any chance you want to be the mistress of my heart, the mistress of my bed and home, the mistress of King's Eden…for all the years ahead of us.''

Relief and joy erased the tension of wretched doubt.

''I'm not asking for a decision,'' he went on. ''I know it's too soon. But I think you understand how it is, that this land is another kind of mistress and you'd have to tolerate its call on me. If you don't see any possibility of sharing what I'd need you to share…''

''I'd share anything with you,'' she cut in fervently. ''Anything!'' She felt him hold his breath and into her mind slipped the words Elizabeth King had spoken of her husband, Lachan, words that held the truth of her feeling for the man holding her in his arms. She hitched herself up, sliding her arms around his neck, speaking directly to the eyes questioning hers. ''*You* are where I want to be. Whatever that entails, Nathan.''

His sigh whispered out through a smile that warmed her entire being. ''So we have a beginning,'' he said, a husky contentment in his voice.

''And no end in sight,'' Miranda answered exultantly.

He laughed and rolled her onto her back, looming over her in a pose of wonderfully dominant maleness. ''I gave you a choice,'' he said teasingly.

''There was no choice,'' she retorted. ''Only you.''

''No one but you,'' he answered softly.

And there was respect for the truths they had spoken this night in the love-making that followed. It was a good beginning, an open and honest communication of where they stood with each other, and Miranda ardently hoped that all the tomorrows would prove they were right in feeling what they did.

CHAPTER SIXTEEN

NATHAN waited in his office for the call he was expecting from Tommy. The weekend was over and he was content he'd made the most of it with Miranda, but he wanted to be sure there would be no comeback from the man who'd driven her into his life in the first place. He was certain now that Hewson was out of her heart, but he wanted her mind clear of him, as well—the past completely past.

It appalled him that he himself had briefly cast Miranda in the role Hewson had maliciously painted—a woman on the make, uncaring whom she hurt. Lies...yet that morning at Cathedral Gorge, he had let his own frustration and her choice of words weave such a false picture.

Completely false.

And he'd hated Hewson for coming up with the same sexual scenario out of spite. All too easy to target a woman who had no back-up. But, by God! there would be no lack of back-up in this instance.

The telephone rang.

He snatched up the receiver, automatically noting the time—8.41—which more or less placed the proposed Monday morning departure on schedule.

"Nathan?"

"Here."

"The Hewson charter flight is lifting off as I speak," Tommy announced smugly. "The birds have flown."

"You saw them onto the plane yourself?"

"No. I sent Sam to do that. I'm watching it from the homestead verandah."

"Dammit, Tommy, I asked you."

"Calm it, brother. No love lost between Sam and the Hewsons. She would have hog-tied them and hauled them into their seats if they'd so much as hesitated. And quite frankly, I'd had enough of them."

"Is the problem cleared?"

"Oh, I think we established a pertinent understanding and Jared will make it stick during their stay in Broome." He chuckled. "By the time Bobby-boy pays out there, I rather fancy he'll want to forget he ever came to King's Eden."

"What payment are we talking about, Tommy?"

"Now, Nathan, you got the kudos for whizzing Miranda out of harm's way. I deserve the kudos for clearing the decks. Bring her back now and I'll tell you all."

The call was disconnected before Nathan could press the point. He hoped Tommy's confidence was not misplaced. A snake had a habit of wriggling and spitting venom even when it was spiked. Still, Tommy should know his own business. It was not only a matter of protecting Miranda. The resort was his baby.

Nathan smiled to himself as he moved out of the office and headed down the hall to Miranda's room where she'd gone to pack her clothes, ready to leave. He didn't mind the resort any more, despite the occasional irritation of tourists wandering where they shouldn't. It had brought him the gold he'd thought he'd never find. True gold. And he'd staked his claim to it. His charming and gregarious brother could win as many kudos as he liked. It wouldn't win Miranda. She was his and his mind was set on keeping her his. Whatever it took.

He knocked on her door, the memory of last night's love-making fresh in his mind. Sleep had been minimal but he didn't feel tired. He'd never felt more vibrantly alive, excitement stirring through him again as she called out, "Come in," the words reminding him of her sexual openness, inviting all he wanted of her and revelling in every intimacy.

He stepped into her room, itching to hold her once more, and the anxious eyes she turned to him spurred him on.

"Is it all right? Have they gone?"

"Yes."

She sagged into his embrace, her arms winding around his neck so the full lush femininity of her was pressed against him. He couldn't resist flattening his palm across the pit of her back, fitting her even closer as he lifted his other hand to stroke away her worry lines.

"Tommy assures me Hewson won't be coming back. It's safe for you to return to the resort."

"How did he handle it?" she asked, uncertainty still clouding her eyes.

"He insists we come and find out." He smiled to reassure her. "Tommy enjoys a bit of boasting."

She sighed, her breasts heaving sensuously. He'd never been so horny in his entire life. Difficult to push temptation aside but it was time for business now and Tommy would not appreciate being kept waiting.

"I just hope there aren't any nasty repercussions," she said, still fretful.

"Not on King's Eden, Miranda," he promised with absolute confidence, and kissed her frown away. "Ready to go?"

"Yes." Trust and courage glowed in her eyes.

His heart kicked into a joyous beat at this further evidence that his instincts had been right all along. It had simply been a matter of breaking through her barriers for her real character to be revealed and everything made sense to him now. Whatever had made Miranda Wade, the result was she was made for him. There was not one response from her that didn't fit want he wanted, what he craved.

With this assurance dancing through his mind, he broke away and picked up her bag. He would take her back to the resort and this tourist season would be long enough for her to know the life she would be taking on with him, but he had little doubt about the choice she would make. It had to be.

He took her hand. She looked at him. It was more than a physical link and she knew it. The bonding was there in her eyes. However many partings there would be, Nathan told himself none of them would change what they were to each other, and his soul filled with happiness at the thought. He would not be walking alone through life. Miranda would walk with him.

The drive back to the resort reminded Miranda of the drive away from it on Friday night...the confusion and fear that had churned through her then. The weekend had certainly sorted out where she stood with Nathan and she could almost bless Bobby Hewson for having unwittingly forced an outcome she hadn't dared to believe in a few days ago. Nevertheless, anxiety still fretted at the edges of her happiness.

She had brought this trouble to King's Eden. Inadvertently, but nonetheless irrevocably. She would feel responsible if Bobby did some damage to the resort's good reputation and she couldn't bring herself to believe he wouldn't. It was impossible to trust the man or his word.

Unlike Nathan. She feasted her eyes on him as he drove, loving every aspect of him. He wasn't just big on the outside. He was big all through. Her skin prickled in sensual delight, just remembering the pleasures they'd revelled in last night, how she'd felt so wonderfully enveloped by him, safe and cossetted, belonging to him and with him.

He hadn't said he loved her, but wanting her to think of sharing his life—all the years ahead of them—and hoping she wanted to be *the mistress of his heart*...why would he crave her love, if he didn't feel love for her? The words would come—she was sure of it—when he felt the time was right. Though she didn't really need until the end of the tourist season to know what she already knew...that nothing was going to change her mind or heart. Nathan was the man for her.

Though she did owe an obligation to Tommy, to work out her contract at the resort...if he wanted her to. It might be better if she didn't, should there be any risk of Bobby spreading damaging lies about the resort because she was the manager. Were Nathan and Tommy right in believing they had fixed the problem?

She hoped so.

It would be good to lay the past to rest, knowing it could never come back to hurt her or those she cared about, and that included everyone who'd supported her at King's Eden. As Nathan drove through the resort to the homestead, she felt she had established herself as a person in her own right here. Maybe that was the effect of the outback, bringing out one's inner resources to meet the challenge of it.

Sam and Tommy were waiting on their arrival, their stances on the homestead verandah reflecting the sparring mood typical of any conversation between them. However, attention was instantly focused on Nathan and Miranda as they alighted from the Land Cruiser. All personal wrangling halted as the *new couple* were scrutinised for sexual signals.

"Well, before I skip off," Sam addressed them, "you'd better tell me if I'm to damp down the rumours or let them fly. That sleazy creep, Hewson, yapped on about Miranda, having her claws into you, Nathan, and I told him flat that if she did, it was precisely where you wanted her claws to be because no one got to you unless you opened up to them."

"How very perceptive of you, Sam!" Nathan answered good-humouredly.

"So?" She gave him a piercing look. "What am I to say?"

"That I take intense pleasure in every one of Miranda's claw-marks and can't wait for more."

"What?" Sam's eyes goggled at Miranda. "You two truly are an item?"

"Yes," she answered, casting a chiding look at the man beside her. "Though I'm not really into clawing."

"Oh, boy, this is good! This is really good!" Sam enthused, then turned an arch look to Tommy who had apparently taken the news with bland equanimity. "Looks like you'll have to make do with Celine thinking you're adorable. And that will only last until she hooks up with Jared in Broome and gets her lustful little hands on him."

"I couldn't give a damn about Celine," Tommy retorted with a bored look. "It was just part of the game."

"And you're *such* a good game player!"

Sam stepped off the verandah and pasted a brilliant smile on her face for Nathan and Miranda. "I'm glad for both of you." She clapped Nathan's shoulder in passing. "I'll try to get Miranda to let her nails grow, Nathan. If ever a man deserves what he wants, it's you."

With that final little snipe at Tommy, she walked off jauntily, leaving him glaring after her.

"One of these days when that little witch gets off her broomstick..."

"You'll beat her with it?" Nathan drily surmised.

Tommy huffed feelingly. "You couldn't even beat submission out of Sam."

"You don't want submission, Tommy," Nathan said knowingly.

It won a crooked smile. "No, but a bit of respect would go a long way." His eyes flashed satisfaction.

"Which is what I taught Hewson. As well as ramming it home that nobody does us a damage without paying a price."

"I haven't had a chance to thank you for taking over for me, Tommy," Miranda breathed, acutely aware of what she owed both brothers.

His face broke into a cheerful grin. "One of the best moments of my life...Nathan actually asking me to stand shoulder to shoulder with him against the enemy. For that alone, you're always going to be special to me, Miranda."

He stepped back and waved them onto the verandah. "Let's go inside and park your bag. Time's moving on. I'll have to be leaving myself in a minute."

"Not before you tell us the nuts and bolts," Nathan said as they entered the homestead.

"Just got to collect my stuff from the office."

"Tommy..."

"Now, Nathan, give me credit," Tommy crowed, wagging an admonishing finger as he headed them towards the hall leading to the administration wing. "I can spin a story better than most."

"True."

"And our guests love outback stories." His eyes twinkled with teasing triumph. "So over dinner on Saturday night, I regaled them with the legend of Lachlan's law."

"Lachlan's law?" Miranda queried.

Tommy waved dismissively. "Nathan can tell you."

"A marked change of attitude on Sunday?" Nathan quizzed his brother.

"Like magic it was," Tommy assured him. "Sam

had the highly questionable pleasure of being the Hewsons' guide all day Sunday, and she reported there was no further mention of Miranda and no digs about management. Of course, I did finish up my story with the reflection that you, Nathan, were made in the same mould as our father and held in the same regard by Albert's tribe.''

"Albert?'' Miranda couldn't help asking, not understanding what the Aboriginal guide and didgeridoo player had to do with this.

"A particularly vivid touch of reality to the story since they'd met him that morning,'' Tommy remarked smugly. He grinned at Nathan. "Then last night I laid the pearls on Celine, shovelling the pitch that her skin was made for them, the perfect sheen for her beguiling perfection, etcetera etcetera and offering up Jared to show her the best in the world. And that, my dear brother, is guaranteed to cost Hewson many, many thousands of dollars.''

"The price of pride!'' Nathan said, and laughed. "I salute you, Tommy. Forget the shoulder to shoulder. You can stand in front of me any time.''

"I shall take that accolade and shove it down Sam's throat on some appropriate occasion,'' Tommy said with relish. "Meanwhile—'' he lowered his brows at both of them as they turned into the administration wing ''—am I going to have to rearrange management here?''

"You can count on one season, Tommy,'' Nathan answered. "The rest is up to Miranda. Her choice.''

"Right!'' he said in some relief, halting at the office

door and gesturing them on to Miranda's private quarters. "I'm off then. No playing on my time, Nathan."

"Your time is much appreciated." A pause for a warm handshake. "Thank you."

"You're welcome."

Tommy disappeared into the office and Nathan walked on with Miranda who was silently rejoicing in how clearly and openly he had declared his interest in her, both to Sam and to Tommy. One season…then the choice was hers. No backing off from him. This wasn't pillow-talk. This was real.

She unlocked her apartment door. Nathan followed her in with her bag, moving to place it on the bed, ready for her to unpack.

"What was Lachlan's law?" she asked, closing the door to seal the privacy she wanted for just a few more minutes before taking up the reins of management again.

He set the bag down and turned around, a curious, assessing look on his face as though wondering how she would react to it. "Our family has a long history of driving serpents out of Eden, Miranda," he said, eerily conjuring up the thought she'd had about Eden on her journey here.

"In the old days, there was no law in these parts, except what we instigated and practised ourselves," Nathan went on. "For any isolated community like a cattle station to work well, a harmony had to be maintained on all levels. That remains true. Always will."

She nodded. "It's true of this resort, too, maintaining a good morale amongst the staff. I appreciate how important it is, Nathan."

"Critical to holding the right balance," he agreed. "The outback strips us of easy escapes. We have to live with what's here. And from the beginning, the Kings forged a close connection to the local tribe of Aborigines. It was of mutual benefit. They were always assured of food and shelter, and having a natural affinity to the land, they were by far the best stockmen we could have working the cattle."

"This is Albert's tribe you're talking about?"

"Yes. Twenty-seven years ago, Albert's father was the foreman at the station, a highly respected tribal elder whom my father trusted to carry through any task. A drifter arrived one day, asking for a job, said he was a trained mechanic. My father set him to work repairing machinery. A few weeks later, when the men were out at the stock-camps, he broke into the supply store, stole a bottle of whisky, got himself drunk, then bashed and raped Albert's mother."

"Oh, no!" Miranda groaned, hating the thought of any woman being so brutally victimised.

"Albert, who was eight at the time, helped her up to the homestead. My mother took her in, and sent both Albert and me out riding for my father. All the men came in because justice had to be seen to be done, especially when it involved a white man against a black woman. The rapist displayed the attitude that any abuse against Aborigines was acceptable and shouldn't be punished."

"How can people think like that?" Miranda cried.

"It was not how any of us thought on the station and if a strong stand wasn't taken on it, there would have been a very serious breach of trust amongst our people. I hope you can see that, Miranda, because King's Eden runs on the understanding—forged through generations—that the Kings look after their people.''

She gave a wry smile. ''Since I've just benefited from that principle, I'm hardly likely to criticise it, Nathan.''

He returned her smile. ''Well, just remember what I'm telling you happened almost thirty years ago, and the justice meted out was for the ultimate good of the community.''

''You're warning me it was harsh?''

''More…primitive. But then the outback is primitive.''

''Go on,'' she urged.

''To teach the man respect for the race he belittled, my father ordered that he be taken out to the most barren section of the King Leopold Range in the middle of the Kimberly, where he was to be left to survive on his own, as the Aborigines had for thousands of years.''

''Did he survive?''

Nathan shrugged. ''The story goes he's still wandering around the wilderness. There have been sightings of a feral white man over the years.''

''Cast out of Eden,'' Miranda murmured.

''He'd destroyed his right to stay. There's a lot of greys we can accommodate, but once the line of respect is abused, appropriate action has to be taken.''

''So that's Lachlan's law.''

''And mine,'' he said quietly.

''I know. And Tommy's. And Jared's. Your father passed it on to all of you, didn't he?''

"As it was passed to him."

Family lore...survival built on support and integrity.

"It's good, Nathan," she said in a burst of heartfelt belief. "I like your world."

His face lit with a smile that grew in warmth as he crossed her sitting area to where she still stood by the door. "I like...*everything* about you, Miranda Wade." He lifted a hand and stroked his finger down the slight cleft in her chin. "Do you feel okay about Hewson now?"

"Yes. He can't win. He won't want to invite more defeat."

"So you feel safe again."

"Very safe."

"I'd better go and let you get on with your work."

"Yes."

"I'll call you tonight."

"Please."

"I hope you keep liking my world, Miranda."

How could she not with him in it? But he kissed her before she could speak, kissed her with slow, beguiling sensuality, with the simmering promise of much more to come...for both of them.

CHAPTER SEVENTEEN

"A WEDDING!" Elizabeth King repeated, trying to contain the delight swelling her heart.

"Yes. Seven weeks from now," Nathan instructed. "The weekend after the resort closes. Will you do it? I know Miranda wouldn't ask but I want it for her. The whole big production…a marquee on the lawn by the river…"

"Nathan, I haven't even heard of an engagement yet. Have you asked Miranda to marry you?"

"Not in so many words. I've been waiting on the ring. Jared brought it with him today."

"You're sure of her answer?"

"Absolutely."

His eyes flashed with an indomitable arrogance that was pure Lachlan, and for a moment Elizabeth was transported back to the night when her husband-to-be told her she was *his* woman, and not to give him any runaround about it because that would just be wasting time better spent together.

"I want you to stand in for her mother, since Miranda no longer has one," Nathan went on. "Do all the wedding arrangements, take her to buy the dress, make her feel like a bride planning her big day. She's had none of the family support we take for granted. I want you to offer it to her tonight, convince her it's what you want, too."

"It is!" Elizabeth laughed in a burst of elation. She'd got it right...bringing Miranda into Nathan's life. It had worked! "My first daughter-in-law..."

"So you'll do it?" Nathan pressed.

"Of course. Any dream Miranda has I'll do my best to fulfil." *Because she will fulfil mine.*

"Good!" Nathan's face lit with satisfaction. "Then what I plan is this..."

Miranda felt increasingly nervous as she drove over to the station homestead for dinner with the King family. She hadn't seen Elizabeth or Jared since the night early in May, when she'd revealed her own lack of family. That was five months ago...five months of learning everything about King's Eden, and loving every minute of it.

But they hadn't witnessed that, hadn't seen as Tommy had, how much she'd taken to this outback life. However, they surely knew of her current relationship with Nathan and Nathan was not about to hide it. Nor did she want him to. Jared's reaction didn't worry her, but Elizabeth's...

Miranda couldn't help wanting her approval. Not that it would change her feelings for Nathan. It would just be so much nicer if his mother could readily accept her as part of Nathan's life. An integral part, Miranda hoped.

He must have been listening for the Jeep to arrive. Miranda had no sooner pulled up beside the bougainvillea hedge, than Nathan was striding down the path. She simply sat and watched him, her man coming to claim her, emanating the force of energy that always entranced her. He collected her from the Jeep, swept her with him onto the verandah, but instead of taking her into the house, led her around to the west side of it.

"What are we doing? Is something wrong?" she asked, apprehension skittering through her.

"Absolutely not." He grinned, the sparkle in his eyes denying any trouble whatsoever. "Just wanted a few private minutes with you. I find that lemon dress very fetching."

She laughed, relaxing against him as he drew her over to the verandah railing. This side of the house faced the river, which was shining like a ribbon of yellow glass, reflecting the last vibrant rays of the sun as it slipped below the horizon. Nathan slid behind her, curling his arms around her waist, rubbing his cheek against her hair.

"A golden river, a golden sky, a golden woman," he murmured.

"And you said you were never romantic," Miranda teased.

"Ah, but I am, when I truly feel it in my heart. Look what I have in my hand, Miranda."

He held it out as she glanced down. It was a grey velvet jeweler's box—a ring box!

Her heart stopped, then catapulted around her chest. Was this it...the commitment of forever?

"Open it!"

The soft pulse of his words in her ear made her dizzy. Her hands trembled as they moved to obey his command. For a moment, the spring lid of the box seemed to resist the pressure of her thumbs and fingers.

Then it opened and she gasped at the splendour of the ring twinkling up at her—a huge oval yellow diamond surrounded by smaller white diamonds, set on a band of gold.

"Wear this and the sun will never set on my love for you, Miranda," Nathan murmured as he lifted the ring from its satin slot. "Will you marry me?"

"Yes," she whispered, spreading her left hand so he could slide the ring onto her third finger. It fitted perfectly. She couldn't stop gazing at it, stunned by the sheer magnificence of his choice for her.

"Do you like it?"

Her heart too full to speak, she whirled around and let her eyes speak for her as she flung her arms around his neck and pulled his head down for all her feelings to be expressed in a kiss. She loved him so much, unequivocally, had done for a long time, and for this proposal to come now, before the season was over…and such a fabulous ring would have been ordered even earlier. Nathan had to believe they were truly made for each other and nothing would ever break the bond they shared.

"I take it that means yes," he said happily, his eyes shining into hers.

"The sun will never set on my love for you, either," she promised huskily. "I'll die with your ring on my finger, Nathan."

He laughed. "I'd rather you marry me first. If it's okay with you, that will be a week after the resort closes."

"Anything you arrange is okay with me," she said blissfully.

"Then let's go and get my mother moving on it."

"Your mother?"

"She never had a daughter. You're it, Miranda. Her first bride in the family. She can hardly wait to arrange a wedding to remember."

"Really?" Miranda had never allowed hope or imagination to zoom that far. "I was worried she might not approve of us."

"*Big* wedding! *Huge* celebration to welcome in the new mistress of King's Eden. Brace yourself for the inevitable, my love! No escape from it."

She didn't want to escape from it. At long last she truly belonged somewhere…to this man, this place, this family…and their wedding would put the final seal on the sense of belonging.

Elizabeth watched them enter the sitting-room, hand in hand, their faces aglow with happiness…a very well-matched couple, she thought with satisfaction. The party of people Nathan had invited to celebrate the engagement thronged around them, showering congratulations and good wishes—all the station community and the friends Miranda had made at the resort, most of them radiating pleasure in the announcement.

Though not quite everyone…

A wistful look on Sam's face, Elizabeth noted. And a touch of envy on Tommy's. Nothing like seeing two people really getting it together to bring home one's lack of success in that area. Perhaps Nathan and Miranda's wedding could be used to promote the match that should have been made years ago, but for two very stubborn and proud personalities.

Tommy as best man.

Sam as chief bridesmaid.

The goodwill of the day rubbing off on them.

Some discreet meddling.

Oh, yes, this was going to be a *big* wedding.

Elizabeth had the next generation of Kings right in her sights!

AUTHOR'S NOTE

THE story you have just read is the first of three revolving around the Kings of the Kimberly—all of them set in outback Australia.

I trust you have enjoyed the journey of love taken by Nathan and Miranda in *The Cattle King's Mistress*.

I hope you will be thoroughly entertained and touched by Tommy and Sam's bumpy road towards marriage in *The Playboy King's Wife*. This book will be available in Presents in the coming months and I promise you it will be a sizzling read!

Emma Darcy

HARLEQUIN *Presents*

Set in the steamy Australian outback
a fabulous new triology by
bestselling Presents author

Emma Darcy

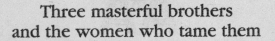

Kings of the
Outback

Three masterful brothers
and the women who tame them

On sale June 2000
THE CATTLE KING'S MISTRESS
Harlequin Presents®, #2110

On sale July 2000
THE PLAYBOY KING'S WIFE
Harlequin Presents®, #2116

On sale August 2000
THE PLEASURE KING'S BRIDE
Harlequin Presents®, #2122

Available wherever Harlequin books are sold.

HARLEQUIN®
Makes any time special ™